THE BLESSED MANY

THE EXTRAORDINARY SERIES

PAM EATON

COOPER AVE PRESS

Editor - Jana Miller

Cover Design - Molly Phipps with We Got You Covered Book Design

ISBN-13: 978-0-9996787-3-2

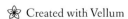 Created with Vellum

For my babies.
Dream big, go after those goals, and know that I love you more than I
thought was possible.

CONTENTS

ONE

My whole body protests as I sit up from my spot on the hard, cold floor. It's tough trying to see in the dark, but I'm...in a kitchen? Maybe? How did I get here? My hands start to tremble and I bring them up in front of my face. They're covered in dirt, dried blood, and who knows what else. *Would you look at that.* Apparently, I lost a whole fingernail. I turn my hand over and back. Shouldn't I be rolling around in agony? I keep looking at my gruesome finger in a sort of detached fascination. It's like someone else's finger. How odd.

A distant noise makes me look up at the counter visible in the moonlight. Is that a phone ringing?

I gingerly stand, listing to the side as I do, and stretch my arm out until my hand touches the vibrating phone on the wall. "Hello," I say into the receiver.

"Rebecca." A stern male's voice says my name.

"That's me."

I hear voices in the background. "Rebecca. It's Mr. Smith." Why does it seem like he's straining for patience? He's the one who called me.

"Were you successful?" he asks.

"Successful?" I don't understand, but my body starts to break out in a sweat like it knows what he's talking about even if my mind doesn't.

"I need to debrief you about your mission. I need to know if it was a success. It'll take hours for someone to come get you. Can you transport to headquarters?"

The word *mission* pings around in my brain.

I shake my head, trying to break up the thick fog clogging it. "What?" I ask. What's he talking about? Why can't I focus on anything?

"I just got off the phone with Gregory. We need you back here."

The word *traitor* whispers through my mind as I register the sound of Gregory's name on someone's lips. And it's like a sledge-hammer to my system. Images flash behind my eyes, and I want to turn away from them but I can't. *Ania running into the throng of soldiers. My body thrown against the gate. Gregory leaning out of the SUV.*

They keep going through my mind like a horror movie on repeat.

I drop the phone and sink to the floor, fisting my hands into my hair.

He left me.

He *left* me.

He left *me*.

Ania's gone. She's dead. Her life for mine.

Tony betrayed us.

I'm stuck in the awful hell of memories on constant loop. The smell of the fresh-turned dirt from the explosion clogs my nose. My body aches with the echo of it slamming into the metal gate. The sound of squealing tires fills my ears, and my vision fills with the image of the SUV leaving me behind. My mouth opens and I let an anguished scream rip through.

Mr. Smith keeps calling my name through the phone on the floor beside me. And it's like one small part of my brain knows I need to answer him, but the majority of my brain won't release me from this endless loop.

I hear the word "shock" yelled, but before I can grab on to any more words or make myself focus, the images flood again, spiraling me farther down into a nightmare I can't escape.

"BECCA." I hear my name close by and I turn towards it.

More sounds start filtering in. Birds are singing in the distance. The scuff of shoes somewhere in the vicinity of my head. The scrape of a chair being pulled out.

"No, don't touch her yet," a raspy voice says.

"Rebecca. Open your eyes," someone commands. Mr. Smith? Only he would demand I make my body do something it doesn't want to.

I slowly open my eyes, but they feel gritty. I blink a few times. Rays of sunlight highlight brown Oxfords right next to my face. I'm on the floor? It's morning? How long have I been here?

I go to turn my head, but everything protests. It feels like I got beat to a pulp. All my muscles scream at me. It's like having a thousand charley horses at once. A groan manages to slip out.

"There you go. Let's see if we can sit you up and get some water in you," Mr. Smith says. He grabs me by my arms and forces my body up and against a cabinet. A bottle of water is shoved in my hand soon after.

I take a sip of water and let my head fall to the side. I get my first glimpse of who pulled out the chair. Guy has to been close to eighty if not older, with his white hair and loose hanging skin. Dark brown age spots cover his cheeks and his bony hands, which rest on top of a cane. With his sweater and loafers, he'd pass for a typical grandfather, except I doubt anyone at Project Lightning could be described as *typical*. His eyes stay trained on me, silently assessing. Probably judging.

Mr. Smith crouches down in front of me, blocking my view of the old guy. His eyes scan down my body, evaluating. "Anything broken?" he asks.

I slowly move my legs and stretch my arms. Everything feels like it's being stabbed by a blunt knife, but it seems like I'm in one piece, at least physically. Mentally is another story. My brain still feels like it's stuck in a fog. And the last twenty-four hours keep looping in my mind, but they don't feel like my memories, more like a bad movie I watched.

"I don't think so," I tell him, my voice hoarse.

He doesn't question me, since I can't lie to him, but his eyes still scan me, maybe seeing something I can't. He shifts to the side a little, making the old guy visible again. "This is Mr. Rivers, my old boss, the previous director of Project Lightning. When this mission went to hell, I called him in. Last thing we need is the North Korean government trying to track you down." His words are cautious, slow.

My eyes lock on Mr. Rivers. He gives me a gentle nod but doesn't say anything. They're both treating me like a wounded animal.

"Do you know what you kept saying into the phone?" Mr. Smith asks carefully.

"No." I have no clue. The last thing I remember is a phone ringing.

"You kept saying 'Tony betrayed us,' over and over again," he tells me.

Tony's name is a shot of adrenaline to my system. My whole body jerks, and both men put their hands out like they could hold me back.

"What happened with Tony?" Mr. Smith asks.

My hands start to shake as I reach out and grip Mr. Smith's shirt sleeve, bringing him closer. I need to get the words out. Someone needs to know. Ania's death can't be in vain. "He was our eyes." The words rush past my lips, and I know my eyes are wild. "And when it was time for us to leave, Ania asked if the coast was clear and he said it was. *He. Said. It. Was.*"

I swallow down the emotion trying to choke me. "He led us into

THE BLESSED MANY   5

the hands of hundreds of soldiers. The line went dead. It was his voice in our ears, and he led us into a trap. Ania ran into the throng of soldiers without a second thought...all so I could escape." His shoulders slump, but only for an instant. If I hadn't been watching him, I would have missed it.

He pries my fingers back from the death grip on his arm and I slump back down. "Are you sure?" he asks.

"It was his voice," I tell him, desperate for him to understand.

"Are all your agents accounted for?" Mr. Rivers asks.

Mr. Smith runs a hand roughly over his hair. "No."

"Sariah?" Mr. Rivers asks.

What does *she* have to do with anything?

"I'm working on tracking her down," Mr. Smith tells him, his voice tense.

Mr. Rivers makes a sound of disappointment. And I'm still sitting here not able to follow their conversation. Mr. Smith turns his face away and I watch as he focuses on something to my right. I follow his eyes and see my backpack, a black box half hanging out. He reaches for it, opens the box, and his whole body slumps after he peeks inside of it. He quickly closes it and hands it to Mr. Rivers.

That box causes pictures to flash in my mind, and this time it's like the movie is skipping. A room filled with computers. My hand grabbing the box. Ania telling me to finish the mission.

Ania.

"You need to call Ania's dad," I tell the room.

"They'll already know, dear," Mr. Rivers says. His voice takes on a soft note.

My body deflates. "Of course," I say. That means Ania's daughter, Bronia, now has the strength of a hundred men. Geez, that poor kid.

The ring of a cell breaks through the tension in the air.

Mr. Smith reaches into his suit coat and pulls out his phone. "Hello," he says.

His eyes flick to me briefly. "She's all right. Coming out of her shock."

Is that what I am? In shock? I shake my head, trying to focus more on his one-sided conversation. "No. I need you there. Something isn't adding up." He pauses. "Yes. I'm going to see if I can get her to go there tomorrow. I'll call you later to let you know."

He ends the call and Mr. Rivers looks at him with raised brows. "Gregory," Mr. Smith says in answer to the unasked question.

My heart stutters at the mention of *that* name. But soon the anger comes with a shot of adrenaline. And it feels so good to be able to feel anything through this fog. So I latch on to it and let the fury race through me, waking up all my nerve endings. I slowly rise to me feet, my hands clenched into fists at my sides. I feel like I could breathe fire right now. "He left me there. He let that SUV pull away. He should have known Tony was going to double-cross us."

"Calm down," Mr. Smith says, trying to force something that isn't going to happen anytime soon.

Seriously? "Why aren't you questioning him? How do you know he didn't betray us as well?" I shout the questions.

"What is my power?" he asks me, his voice calm, controlled.

Why is he asking that? Why isn't he demanding more information? Why isn't he as furious as I am?

"Becca, he can't lie to me," Mr. Smith says, his voice taking on a sharp tone.

"Right," I say, some of my anger lessening. And Gregory might not be able to lie to Mr. Smith, but Gregory had no problem lying to me.

"We need to get back to headquarters and have the doctor check you out. Make sure nothing happened during the blast."

"But what about Tony?" I ask.

"I'm hoping I can get you to transport back to the spot where you dropped off Tony and scope the area out. I've also got some agents en route that should be able to help. First, let's make sure you're okay, get some food into you and have you rest. Tomorrow we'll see what we can do."

I pick my coat up off the floor and the letter Ania wrote for Bronia pokes out a bit. That's another thing I'm going to have to tackle, but not right now. I promised her I would deliver it, and I won't break my word.

I follow the two men out of the cabin and into a waiting black town car. My eyes stay glued on the cabin as we pull away. We spent such a short time there, but the memories slam into me with such force my stomach cramps. Lying on the roof with Tony. Working in the woods with Ania. Sitting on that front porch with Gregory. I make myself face forward, and I work to build the walls I'll need to keep myself sane. Because not only do we need to figure out what happened with Tony, but I have to prepare myself to face Gregory. And if I want to survive that, I'll need to guard my heart.

This place changed my life, but as we drive away, I wish I had a match the burn it all down.

TWO

I stand in front of the door to the cafeteria, debating. While my stomach is making itself perfectly clear that it wants me to go in there, everything else rebels. Everyone will be in there eating dinner, and I don't think I can handle the stares. Scratch that—I know I can't handle them. If the doctor hadn't ordered me to get food after he examined me, I'd be back in my room. I know I need to eat; my stomach is howling like a sad husky. But what about all the questions they're going to ask me? I have no clue how to answer them, but at least the good doctor shot me up with some anxiety meds, so I'm basically coasting right now.

All right. I can do this. And maybe if I keep telling myself that, it'll make it easier.

I open the double doors and walk in. I wait for a moment—for what, I have no clue. It's not like they're going to tackle me. Hopefully.

My eyes zero in on the buffet line. Maybe I can just grab some food and take it back to my room.

I move towards it and a hand clamps on my shoulder, causing me to do a whole body flinch. I spin to see Mike, one of the other trainees who started here at Project Lightning with Tony and me, standing behind me. He's still as big as an ox, but I swear he's gotten bigger. And judging by the confusion on his face, I might have flickered when I flinched. He shakes his head and refocuses on my face. "You're back again?" he asks, seeming genuinely curious.

I shrug off his hand. "I just got here."

I don't know what I can tell him, but I have a feeling that I need to keep my lips sealed. "Is Tony with you?" he asks, looking towards the doors.

My whole body stiffens. "No, it's only me."

His body slumps forward and he loses a few inches in height, if that's even possible. Even though Tony and I were only here a short time before going to the cabin, I know those two bonded.

"Is he coming back soon?" he asks. His voice is flat. Not cocky and sure like before.

"I don't know." I can't believe I'm about to ask this, but... "Are you all right?" This is not the guy I met back in orientation, the one who couldn't stop bragging about what an amazing athlete he is. Now he looks like someone kicked his dog.

He shrugs his shoulders.

"Umm, do you want to eat with me?" I ask, surprising myself and him. But the guy looks so dejected.

He nods his head and shuffles his feet behind me as we grab some food and head towards a table.

"Is Sariah out on a mission or something?" I ask him. I remember Mr. Smith and Rivers talking about her, but I can't remember what they said exactly.

Without Sariah here reigning over everything, the room feels different. People still look at me, shocked I'm back, but their stares don't feel like daggers. That negative energy must have left when she did. "I think they sent her out on a mission or something. One day she was here and the next she was gone, just like you guys," he tells me, and it's not hard to miss the jealousy in his voice.

"So, how's it been going?" I try to find something to ease the awkwardness.

"Same old same old, basically like being in prison."

It's probably sucked being stuck here for weeks on end. I got to go to the cabin and breathe the fresh air; everyone else got stuck here. Are they even allowed outside? Maybe that's a dumb question.

We sit for a few more minutes in silence. Waves of depression are crashing off of him; this is so weird. Between the two of us, I would have thought I'd be the more depressed one. But it's as if all the confidence and bravado has been sucked out of him by these sterile white walls.

I take a bite of salad, but the sound of glass shattering at the next table over makes everything seize within me. Suddenly I'm not sitting with Mike anymore, but running through that compound in North Korea. Shouts and screams echo around me. I slap my hands over my ears, desperately trying to block out the sound. Trying to hide from it.

Hands grab my shoulders as someone shouts my name, but the pressure is gone within an instant. Silence reigns. I open my eyes to see I'm back in the cafeteria, not North Korea, but everyone is staring at me. "You—you just—disappeared." Mike stammers out the words.

I push away from the table, my chair crashing to the ground. I look around and see everyone watching me with open mouths. I need to leave. Now.

I race out of the room and into the hall. I close my eyes and my body feels like it's being pulled through a tight spot. I open my eyes and I'm next to my bed. I fall face down on top of it, my heart still racing a mile a minute, sweat pouring off me. I turn my head on my pillow and try to breathe in and out slowly.

What did I just do? Did they all see? Did I flicker? Mike saw. They all saw.

I keep trying to breathe like the doctor said, but I'm too amped up. I grab the small envelope of pills out of my pocket. He said to only take these if I really needed them. Right now I need them. I throw them in my mouth and swallow them down.

THE BLESSED MANY   11

I wish I was with Grandpa. And I wish for the oblivion of sleep to take me. I hope these pills are fast acting.

———————

GRANDPA'S SITTING in one of his big leather chairs in his office, holding picture frames of me and my dad. It's been too long since I've heard his voice. It's been even longer since I've seen him. A lightness infuses my heart to see him again, even if it's only in a dream.

I sit down in the matching leather chair next to him and he drops the picture of me from kindergarten. He grabs the arms of his seat and a curse escapes his lips. "Becca, what on earth are you doing here? I didn't even hear you come in the door." He looks to his office door and back to me.

A sad smile graces my face. "It's just a dream."

He shoots towards the end of his chair and grabs my hand and squeezes it, hard. "It certainly is not a dream."

I look down at my hand, feeling his tight hold on me. But this has to be a dream. I collapsed in bed only moments ago. I search his eyes and the room. "I took the sleeping pills the doc gave me."

He tightens his grip on my hand and the pain radiating up my hand finally convinces me. "Well, I'm not sleeping, and I don't think you are either. And if you just took sleeping pills, it'll take a bit for them to kick in."

I stare into his eyes for a beat, and then I lunge from the chair and throw my arms around him. "I miss you so much. I miss home."

He rubs my back in a slow, soothing motion. "How did you get here?"

I forgot that he doesn't know. I left home before we knew what my powers even were. I transported here once before, but unlike this time, I'd done it on purpose. He might have felt my presence in the room, but I never let him see me. There's no point in lying to him now. He might be the only soul in this world I can completely trust. I drop to the floor, sitting next to his feet and leaning against his legs.

"Grandpa, I can transport myself to anywhere I want in the world. I just need to focus and see it in my mind."

He looks down at me, his eyes wide. And before I can stop it, more incomprehensible word-vomit comes out of my mouth. "It's been hell. We went on assignment. And everything went wrong. Ania told me that my mom was clean before she died. She told me that my mom was murdered. These people knew my dad. Ania—" Heaving sobs threaten to escape, but I put my forehead on his knee, struggling to control them.

His hand smooths over my hair as I try to calm myself. I take a deep breath and force the words past my lips. "Ania died."

His hand stops in my hair at my words. He places a finger to my chin, putting a little pressure so I'll turn and face him. "I'm sorry, sweets," he says, his voice tender.

Tears slip down my check, and he reaches out to catch some of them with his finger.

The phone on his desk rings, and we both turn and stare at it. "Does anyone know you're here?" he asks, his voice quiet.

I look up at him. "No. I've been in my dorm room. I didn't even plan on coming here."

We both watch it, neither of us moving, until it stops.

He releases my chin and drags a hand over his face. "Good. That's probably for the best."

"Okay?" I'm not following him.

He stands up, causing me to stand with him. "Do you want to come home?"

I haven't told him about the kidnappings, or the other agents being murdered. He's already worried about me; can I even add to that? Would coming home put my grandparents in danger too?

"I'll be okay," I say, hoping to convince him, and myself, of that.

He looks so conflicted. He's always been my protector, but I think we're both coming to realize that he can't be that anymore. I don't know if there's anyone who can protect me anymore. I'm on my own in that now.

"You need to get back. But as soon as you can, come home and see me." He brings me into a tight hug. "I love you. Don't you forget that. This is your home, and if you need to come back, you do."

I hug him back as tightly as I can. "I love you too."

I step back and close my eyes, picturing my bed in the dorm room. My body feels the pull of the transport, and soon I can no longer feel the warm air of Grandpa's office, but instead the stiff sheets on my bed.

I keep my eyes closed, and eventually the sleeping pills from earlier kick in, dragging me into much-needed sleep.

"YOU NEED TO SEE THIS THROUGH."

I turn my head from gazing at the striking blue sky to look at Mom beside me in the lush green grass. It's the same place she's visited me before. A strong wind rushes by us from the north, and the brisk coldness of it makes me shiver. We don't have much time. Apparently this is going to be a short dream tonight. The cold always heralds the end of the dream. Not that I really mind if it's short.

A long exhale escapes my lips. She's right. I know there are people counting on me now. But... "What do I need to do? How can I know who to trust anymore at Project Lightning?" I ask her, my voice pleading for someone, anyone, to tell me what to do.

There were two people there I would have trusted with my life, but now Ania is gone and Gregory lied to me.

She places her arm around my shoulder. I stiffen at first but then tell myself to relax. It's still hard to be near her. She gives me a sad smile and removes her arm. "Stick it out, or you'll be hunted down. Just like I was."

Ania told me, right before we raced up the cement ramp, that my mom was murdered.

Still lost in thought, I don't notice my mom getting up and walking back to the hill she came from. "Wait, what do you mean, you were hunted down?" I call after her.

Her voice is warm and calm when she responds. "It's not the time for that story. Keep listening to Mr. Smith for now. I love you, Becca. I'm so proud of you."

I watch her walk over the hill and disappear into the unknown. I stay in the grass, running my fingers through it as if it were hair. And then I rip it out.

The wind whips at my back. The sky's quickly losing its brilliance. An inky color stains it now. I close my eyes.

THREE

There's a persistent knock at the door. I rub the sleep out of my eyes and swing my legs off the bed. My body protests a bit at the movement. My eyes catch the time on the clock next to my bed. Ten o'clock in the morning. Man, I slept over twelve hours?

The knock hasn't stopped, so I quickly move from the bed and open the door. A middle-aged woman stares back at me. Her brown hair is pulled into a tight bun that pinches her face, and her clothes remind me of a stereotypical secretary. "Rebecca?" she asks, plastering on a bright smile that doesn't really reach her eyes.

I lean against the doorframe—of my assigned room—but I won't point that out to her. "That's me."

"Hi. I'm Chelsea, Mr. Rivers's assistant." Guess I got the secretary thing right. She reaches out her hand, and as I reach out mine to shake hers, I feel what most people would think is static electricity but is really the telltale sign of one of the hundred.

"Mr. Smith asked if I'd come get you and escort you to his office." She's still got that smile on her face.

"Let me change real quick," I tell her.

I close my door and lean my forehead against it for a moment. I'm going to need to transport for him. And even though I worked so hard to do it seamlessly, I'm still on edge.

I grab some fresh clothes and throw them on. As I head for the door I stumble over my dirty clothes on the floor, kicking my pants in the process. A gold coin skids across the room. I reach down and pick it up. Mom's sobriety coin. I run my thumb over the raised surface before stuffing it in my pocket. *Later*, I tell myself. I'll think about what this coin means later. And soon I'm stepping out of my room and closing my door.

We walk down the hall together, but I keep my eyes averted, hoping to avoid conversation. "Were you sleeping?" she asks. I guess my aversion tactics suck. "It took you a bit to answer the door."

"Yeah," I say, but leave out any details. I don't know this lady, and I'm not about to tell her I was basically in a drug-induced coma because I freaked out in the cafeteria.

She makes a humming noise, but thankfully we walk the rest of the way in silence.

When we approach Mr. Smith's door, Chelsea walks right in. I hesitate for a moment and follow after her.

Mr. Smith and Mr. Rivers both look up from whatever they're looking at on Mr. Smith's desk as we walk in. His desk is still a mess of papers and folders. My eye catches on the picture of soldiers. Something is always familiar about it, but I haven't figured out why yet. It's hard to make out the faces since they're all wearing helmets.

"Good, you're here. We're just about to contact Gregory via video chat," Mr. Smith says. I cringe at the mention of Gregory. And the anger from earlier flares. But I tamp it down. I haven't let myself think about him yet. I can't do it. How could he not tell me that he could read minds? That's kind of a big thing to leave out when you're supposedly falling in love with someone. How am I ever going to trust him again?

"Gregory filled us in on his perspective on what occurred during the mission. Are you sure that it was Tony giving you directions?" Mr. Smith asks. I shake off thoughts of Gregory.

I don't even have to think about his question; I already know the answer. "Yes, it was definitely him. I would know his voice anywhere."

"Gregory assures us that Tony wasn't planning anything that would allude to double-crossing us. If anything, his thoughts were only about you and worrying that you wouldn't make it out alive."

I try not to blush, but I can feel the heat reaching my cheeks. Mr. Rivers lets out a not-so-subtle cough and I swallow down my embarrassment. "Did it sound like someone was forcing him?" Mr. Smith asks.

"No. He sounded in control," I insist. "And it was his voice. No one can..."

A memory rushes to the front of my mind. I was lying on the roof of the cabin with Tony. We talked briefly about the powers of the others, and he mentioned something to do with Sariah—and her power to take on the voice of anyone. "He wasn't alone, was he?" I ask, staring into Mr. Smith's eyes.

He nods his head.

"Sariah." I say her name like an accusation.

"Possibly. Four days ago, she walked out of here without anyone knowing. And no one knows where she is. She's the only person who could pull this off. We're pretty sure she's the one who led you into the trap, but there's a recording I'm waiting on so we can confirm that."

"How does someone just walk out of here?" There are cameras everywhere.

He rubs a hand over his face before he drops it back down to grip the desk. "We're not sure." Oh, I'll bet it was super hard for him to say those words. "But she had to have had help."

"Okay, so?" I'm not following.

"When I talked with Gregory last night—" A beeping sound cuts him off. Mr. Smith turns and pushes a button on his desk. A 3-D image appears and it's Gregory's face.

Part of me is happy to see he's safe with my own eyes. But mostly I'm pissed.

"Becca," he says my name in a way that's a little too intimate. "You have no idea how glad I am to see you safe."

"You mean unlike when you left me running from soldiers down a road in some town in North Korea while you drove away like it was nothing?" The larger, pissed-off part of me is apparently in charge right now and causing me to speak before even thinking.

The fact that his face only shows shock right now tells me pretty quickly that mind reading only works in person. Because the number of curses and creative insults I'm throwing at him in my mind should be making him flinch.

"It wasn't what—"

Mr. Smith waves his hand in front of the image of Gregory, cutting him off.

"Enough. You two can discuss this later," Mr. Smith tells us.

"Yes, sir," Gregory says.

Mr. Smith stares at him for a moment longer. "Mr. Rivers and his assistant, Chelsea, are present." He points to them behind my shoulder. I totally forgot they were here. Wonderful, they got to witness my little temper tantrum.

Gregory nods.

"Chelsea, can you go see if Xavier and Raven have arrived?" Mr. Rivers asks, and she leaves the room without comment.

"Now, we're keeping you in South Korea for the time being," Mr. Smith tells Gregory. "But I'm going to have Becca transport to Tony's lookout spot."

"I can go there," Gregory says.

Mr. Smith shakes his head. "No. The area's security is too tight right now. Becca can get in and out faster than you."

How come no one's asking me if I want to go back? The idea alone has me sweating like crazy.

"You up for that, Becca?" Gregory asks. Apparently I'm not good at hiding my nerves well.

"Do I really have a choice?" I ask the room.

"Tony is missing," Mr. Smith says. "And I don't know where he is or what's happening to him. Plus, this might lead us to the missing children."

He slides three pictures across the desk. Three little faces look back at me: two little boys and one girl. They all have huge smiles on their faces, and they're all so young. A pain pierces my heart. What are their parents going through right now?

"Their families are devastated. We need to find them too," Mr. Smith says. And just like that, any nerves I have fly out the window. These kids need me. Tony needs me. And he would do whatever it took to find me.

I look into Mr. Smith's eyes. "I'll do it."

"Good. You'll leave later this afternoon. We'll all meet back here at three to see what you found."

I WRING MY HANDS, trying to get the tension out. I've only transported across the world twice. Once by total accident to Poland, and the other...I was able to funnel all my rage, fear and frustration through me so I could get out of North Korea. Though if I keep freaking myself out, I don't know if I'll be able to do this. *Deep breath.*

I shut my eyes and try remembering the spot where I last saw Tony. I remember wishing I had a camera because the view was so beautiful. Images of white-peaked mountains, lush trees with their leaves turning bright autumn colors, and the blue sky flood my mind. I picture Tony, standing outside of the vehicle, talking with Gregory.

The familiar pull of my body transporting envelops me, and before I even have a chance to open my eyes, a strong late fall breeze hits me. I'm back; I'm really here. The sun is barely starting to rise. And while that's beautiful, I don't want to stay here any longer than necessary. As it is, I can feel the same hysteria from earlier building, and it's taking everything in me not to break down.

Breathe.

I look around, hoping something will pop out at me. I trace the ground with my eyes and finally spot a set of footprints left in the dirt. I follow them along path that ends near a cliff. I search the ground, praying for something, anything, that will help us.

"What is that?" I mumble to myself as I look closely at the boulders. *Is that blood?* My heart rate begins to accelerate at the sight of what I'm pretty sure is blood splatter. There are a lot more footprints mixed in with the drops of blood. But what makes me sick to my stomach is the large pool of blood, and the drag marks leading away from it.

This changes everything.

I follow the blood trail for a couple of yards. It stops abruptly, right next to a set of tire marks. "What did they do to you, Tony? Where did they take you?" I ask quietly, looking at the tire tracks.

I follow the tracks a bit, but they lead down the mountain. I trace my steps back, scanning the ground for anything else, but there's nothing else for me to find. I close my eyes and think of Mr. Smith's office, his desk filled with papers, and where he and Mr. Rivers were in the room before I left.

I open my eyes and see Mr. Rivers standing next to the wall. The only thing that gives away the fact that I startled him is the fleeting widening of his eyes.

I look at Mr. Smith and tell him all that I found. Gregory's holographic face still hovers over the desk. No one speaks for a moment, and the silence is extremely uncomfortable. Mr. Smith leans over his desk. "Are you sure there was nothing else there?"

I shake my head. "I looked, but I couldn't find anything else."

I feel like I'm letting everyone down. Aside from following those tire tracks down the mountain, there wasn't anything else there I could have found.

"All right, I'm bringing in extra help anyway," Mr. Smith says.

There's a knock at the door and Mr. Smith tells whoever it is to enter. A petite woman comes prancing—yes she's really prancing—

into the room, smacking gum in her mouth. She's maybe in her thirties, and she's dressed for a day of shopping in tight jeans, a hot pink sweater, and black high-heeled boots. Her straight black hair falls to her waist, and her bronze skin is flawless. She's an agent? And what's with the upbeat attitude? Does she not know why she's here?

Behind the gum smacker, a guy enters the room. His plaid shirt hugs his muscular arms and his jeans are definitely well worn. He moves with ease and complete silence. It's kind of crazy how he makes no noise. His hands are tucked in his front pockets, showing off his dark, whiskey-colored muscular forearms. He shoots me a shy smile as he walks over to Mr. Smith. He's definitely cute.

"Becca, I'd like you to meet two fellow agents, Raven and Xavier." Mr. Smith motions towards them.

Raven beams at me and thrusts her hand out. I hesitate for a moment and reluctantly grasp her hand. "I'm so excited to be working with another girl! I'm always surrounded by so much testosterone. This will be great!" Raven's practically bouncing on her toes. And it's a little much.

At first I don't know why her happiness is pissing me off. But then she smacks her gum once more, and it snaps something in me. "Do you not know that you're here because someone died and someone else was kidnapped?"

Raven takes a step back from me. A small part feels bad for my harsh words, but I can't shake the anger that's been simmering in me.

"Becca, that's enough," Mr. Smith reprimands me. "You aren't the only one who lost Ania. And we all want to find Tony."

"But you haven't even talked about her! And I know her family knows, but what about calling them to give them comfort? What about retrieving her—her—" I can't say the word *body* out loud. It hurts too much. And I can feel the tears streaking down my face, but I don't make a move to wipe them away.

A warm hand clasps mine, jarring me out of my tirade. I look up into Xavier's kind eyes. "I want you to know I'll do all I can to help find out what happened to Tony. And Ania was my friend. I won't rest until we avenge her." His grasp on my hand tightens when he says her name. His voice is deep but soothing, and he looks straight into my eyes, letting me see his honesty.

"Thank you," I whisper.

"Are you good?" Mr. Smith asks, but it feels more like he's asking if I have my crap together.

I turn and locks gazes with him. "Yes," I say, my voice firm.

He holds my stare a moment longer. "Good. I'll be in contact with Ania's father soon. And with the kidnappings, it's even more important that we make sure Ania's daughter is okay.

"The plan is for the three of you to travel back to North Korea and meet up with Gregory. Obviously, this might be a problem with Becca's recent escape from the military compound."

He moves over to his desk and sits down. "All right, let's talk about how we plan to find Tony, and the reason Raven and Xavier are here. We need to get back to North Korea, and quickly," he tells the room.

"But they probably left that area already. Especially with the explosions," I say.

"That's where the rest of us come in," Gregory says.

Mr. Smith points his pen at Xavier. "Xavier's ability has to do with tracking. He can touch the earth where an event happened, and as long as it's within the last three days, he can see what occurred at that spot and help track from there."

Whoa. That's helpful.

"Can't he go to like Sariah's room here and see what happened with her? See if she's involved?" I ask.

"She left over three days ago; it's been too long," Mr. Smith tells us.

"Could that mean someone knows what we're doing now and where we're going?" I ask, my voice rising, because did she know when to leave here?

"The only people who know about *this* mission are in this room now. So if something goes wrong, there won't be many places to look.

But I trust everyone in this room," Mr. Smith tells me, trying to calm me.

I take a deep breath. All right, there are only six of us here. And one used to be the guy in charge of this division.

Mr. Smith points at Raven. "Raven's power is to talk with animals." Holy...she's like a living, breathing Snow White. No wonder she's so peppy; she's living a real life Disney movie on a regular basis.

"Hopefully there will be some animals that were present when Tony was taken," Raven tells us, a little bit more subdued—probably because of my freak-out.

"That's the hope. But now, I want to play for you all the last transmission we have with Tony. Let me know if he sounds off to you," Mr. Smith says, pressing a button on his desk.

"Do you have eyes on the girls?" Gregory asks.

"Yeah, they just left out of the side door," Tony says.

"Is the coast clear?" Ania asks.

"The soldiers are still busy with the civilians, and you have a clear shot to the fence," Tony says.

Why does he sound almost monotone?

"There's over a hundred soldiers up there...Tony? Come in, Tony, are you there?" Ania asks.

Screams are heard over the line.

"What's that? Gregory asks.

"Tony? Tony, where are the girls? Tony!?" Gregory's screaming now.

A large boom echoes across the speakers, and it's like a switch is thrown in my brain.

Flashes of explosions skate across my vision. Distorted screams echo in my ears. The smell of smoke clogs my nose. Metal presses against my face.

"Becca, come on, come back to us," someone pleads with me from a distance.

I claw at the arms pinning me down to the gate at the compound.

I have to leave. I have to meet Gregory. Ania told me to finish the mission.

"Please come back," I hear at a distance. And it's *that* voice that finally penetrates the memories.

My eyes blink rapidly as I try to get rid of the horrific images and concentrate on what's in front of me. The room comes back into focus, but I'm not sitting in my chair anymore. I'm sprawled on the floor; Xavier's holding my arms and Raven has my legs pinned. Gregory's face still hovers over Mr. Smith's desk. He's got one hand gripping his hair, his eyes frantic. "Becca?" Gregory asks.

I take a deep breath. "I'm here," I say, my voice hoarse.

Xavier squeezes my arm reassuringly and then both he and Raven release me. I let myself lie there long enough to take a deep breath. Then I climb back into my chair and keep my eyes trained on the table. My heart is still beating out of my chest, but I keep trying to breathe.

"Can you handle this?" Mr. Smith asks, and I look up into his probing eyes.

I don't have a chance to answer him because Gregory's voice comes booming across the room. "Can she handle this?" he shouts. "Has she even talked to anyone about what happened? Has anyone even mentioned PTSD to her?" He's looking at Mr. Smith and his voice rises with every question.

"Enough," Mr. Rivers says in an eerily calm voice. But everyone comes to attention at it, even Gregory. I keep forgetting the old man is even in the room. "Time is a luxury we don't have right now."

He's right, we don't have time. But can I handle it? I just went back looking for Tony and I didn't break down. Is there really any rhyme or reason behind what triggers me? Is it going to happen again? But I think the most important question I've got to ask myself is, *do I really have a choice if I want to help save Tony?*

"I can do this," I tell Gregory, and shift my gaze to the others in the room so they understand I'm confirming this to all of them. "And

I don't think that was Tony. It was his voice, but it sounded monotone. Tony is full of life. That voice was void of it."

I look back at the image of Gregory hovering over the desk. He nods once like he believes me, like he gets me.

I do my best to shake off the nerves still coursing through me and stand, facing Mr. Smith. "When do we leave?" I ask.

"Raven and Xavier will leave within the hour. You'll meet up with them and Gregory tomorrow," Mr. Smith tells me. He looks back at Gregory. "I'll contact you soon with their flight information," he tells him, then he presses a button and Gregory's face disappears.

Mr. Smith opens a drawer in his desk. He pulls out a box. "You need to this," he says as he hands it to me.

I open it, finding a phone inside. My eyes dart back up to his. I haven't been allowed a phone since getting here.

"We should have given you one earlier. It's pre-programmed with important numbers. Full access to the internet and satellite connections. You should be able to use this anywhere on the planet."

I put the phone in my pocket and it clinks against my mom's sobriety coin.

"Xavier and Raven, check in when you get to your first layover. Becca, get some food and rest. I'll see you in the morning." Mr. Smith dismisses us, and we get up and leave his office.

FOUR

As the three of us leave Mr. Smith's office and walk down the hallway I stop and block Raven's way. Her bubbly expression from earlier is now severely subdued. And while that's honestly not such a bad thing, how I acted with her wasn't okay.

I look up into her searching eyes. "I'm sorry for earlier," I tell her. "It's just—"

"I get it," she interrupts. "Becca, you're young. It wasn't until I hit my twenties that I experienced anything bad on a mission."

"I don't feel young anymore," I tell her, being completely honest.

Her face softens. "Sadly, that's part of this job. We're forced to grow up quickly. And unfortunately, you'll have to learn to cope with things the average person never will. But don't let that ruin who you are. Right now it's hard to image a life outside of these missions, but you'll have to find a way to separate yourself. It'll never get easier, especially when you lose someone. But you've got to remember to live, because that's what Ania would have wanted you to do."

Even though her words ring true, I'm not ready for them. The wound is too fresh. But those words make me breathe a little bit easier, even if it's only a fraction.

I break off from them and head to my room. I wish I could fly with them, but there's a chance that my face is plastered all over North Korea. At least I won't have to endure sitting on a plane that long again.

But there is somewhere I need to go now. I swing by my room and pick up Ania's letter, then I pull out my new phone and plug in the address on the envelope. An aerial photo shows the house. I hold the envelope in one hand and the phone in the other so I can see both the address and satellite photo. I made a promise to her and I won't let her down. I close my eyes and keep the images in my mind.

I open my eyes to see I actually made it to Ania's backyard. A wooden swing set sits in the middle of the yard, and a pink bike rests against the house. Chalk is scattered around the back patio. The breath in my lungs catches and I release it on a harsh breath. They would already know she's gone. Bronia would have received her powers.

I have more in common with Ania's daughter than I care to admit. But at least her mom loved her enough to leave a note, unlike mine.

I jog up the back steps and raise my hand to knock on the screen door, but my hand freezes. There's still time for me to leave. I shake my head and knock. This is important. Part of me hopes no one will answer. I'm not ready for the questions. I don't know how to keep the promise of watching after her daughter.

Heavy footsteps trudge towards the door. My heart pounds in my chest.

The door swings open and a monster of a man fills the frame. I take a hesitant step back.

Black eyes framed by bushy eyebrows pin me to my spot. "Can I help you?" His voice is heavily accented and sounds like gravel scraping down his vocal cords.

"My name's Becca."

He crosses his arms over his barrel chest. "I'm Walter. What can I do for you, Becca?"

I reach into my coat pocket and retrieve the letter. I hold it out to him and my hand wavers. "Ania was one of my mentors. She asked me to deliver this."

He releases a pain-filled breath, and the beast of a man in front of me completely deflates. He reaches for the letter and tenderly traces the inscription on the envelope. "*Robaczku*," he whispers. He clears his throat a few times. "Why don't you come in?" he asks. The grief in his voice almost undoes me.

I look at the door and then back to the yard, where the lonely pink bike sits. He's going to want to know what happened. I can't tell him with Bronia around. She doesn't need to hear this. "Maybe we should talk out here where Bronia can't hear us?" I ask.

He turns and looks into the kitchen. "Let's go have a seat at the picnic table."

I sit down and brace for his questions. I don't even know what I can tell him, but he deserves as many truths as I can give him. "We haven't heard from Mr. Smith, but we obviously know something happened." The sorrow in his voice pierces me.

I still can't believe Mr. Smith hasn't contacted them. I know a lot is going on, but Ania's worked with Project Lightning for so long. I'm going to give this family the closure they need.

I take a deep breath, because he might hate me after I tell him that Ania sacrificed herself for me. I look into his eyes and say a silent prayer for strength. "We were on a mission to retrieve a package. But our escape route was compromised. We were betrayed," I tell him, trying to give as few details as possible with as little emotion as possible.

"She caused a distraction so I could leave with the package." Tears stream down my face. Guess I can't do this without the emotion. "Her life for mine." I won't tell him how. I already had to do that, and I can't let another person have that picture in their mind.

Walter's face contorts in agony. It's one thing to know a loved one died; it's another to hear how it happened. Is he going to hate me? The thought sends my heart careening to the depths of my stomach.

"Please don't hate me." My voice comes out small and weak, and I hate it.

His mouth firms and he grabs for my hand across the table. "How could I hate you? You had no idea any of this would happen. Becca, you're still a child. None of this is your fault. Ania did the honorable thing, and for that I am proud of her. I've always been proud of her. Her mother, Magdalena, was too."

Child? Any childhood innocence was lost a while ago. His words lessen some of the burden I've been carrying about Ania, but that burden is still there.

I take a deep breath. "How's Bronia doing?" I want to smack myself. Stupid question.

"Bronia's ten, so she knew already that she'd have powers one day, but we never thought it would be so soon. Nothing prepares you for losing your mother, though." His face softens. "But you already know that."

I shift uneasily on the bench. This is still an area I don't like to talk about.

"I thought we had years before we'd have to drag Bronia into this world. I had to take her out of school."

Pictures of a ten-year-old hulk destroying her classroom flash in my mind. I can't even imagine.

"I'm waiting for Mr. Smith to come and claim her." His voice is filled with disgust when he mentions Mr. Smith, but his comment makes my arms flood in goose bumps.

He needs to hide. I think of my mother's warnings, Grandpa's recent unease, and the traitors lurking within Project Lightning. They can't stay here.

"I think you guys need to hide," I tell him.

His whole body stiffens like he's on high alert. "Why would you suggest that?" he asks me.

I see Sariah in my mind. If she was able to infiltrate our mission, who else might be a traitor at headquarters? "I don't think Project Lightning is safe. I think there are things going on we don't know about. One of my friends there was kidnapped." I hesitate, because I know I'm not supposed to be telling him these things. "Some of the other agents' kids have been kidnapped, and they're even younger than Bronia. And with what happened with Ania..." I trail off, because nothing more needs to be said about her.

He looks back to the house.

"Could you even go into hiding?" I ask, and he turns back towards me at my question.

He rolls his shoulders, and something like resolve settles on his face. "Yes. My parents survived WWII in Poland. They made sure that we could flee and hide in case anything happened like that again. They taught me well. We'll leave soon."

"Do you know where you'll go?" Part of me is relieved he's taking me seriously, but how can you hide from the FBI?

"My wife made some contacts during a mission in Russia. There's one I'll call on, a good friend; he'll know how to help as well."

His eyes focus back on me, and they soften the way my grandfather's do. "You need to be careful, Becca. It's not safe for you either. Maybe you should come with us."

I think of Tony, of Gregory even though I'm mad at him, of the kids going missing and ending up dead, and I think of Ania's sacrifice. "I can't right now. I need to find my friend. Plus I have a pretty good escape plan."

I close my eyes. And it's barely the blink of an eye before I'm standing behind him with a smirk on my face. He whirls around at my tap on his shoulder. His hand flies to his chest, clutching at it as he mutters some Polish words that I'm pretty sure are curses.

"See, I'll be fine."

"I can see that, but don't become too arrogant. That could lead to your undoing." He lectures me like I'm his grandchild too.

I place my hand on his shoulder to reassure him, then suddenly the back door flies off its hinges, crashing to the cement.

I spin around, waiting for a threat, but all I see is a sad little girl who's the spitting image of Ania, and it robs me of air. "Bronia," I whisper.

She stares at me for a moment, but her eyes look at the door and then move to Walter. "I'm sorry, JaJa," she says, her words full of guilt.

He motions for her to come to him. He opens his arms and she starts toward him. "Gentle," he cautions her softly.

She slowly leans her body against his. And my heart aches because I can tell she wants to throw herself into her grandpa's arms, but with her newfound strength, she could very well hurt him until she learns to control it. "It's okay, *robaczku*. We'll fix the door. It'll take time to handle your strength," he tells her softly, running his hand over her hair. She nods her head against his chest, but her hands are still fisted against her sides.

She pulls back and looks at me. "This is Becca. She—" His voice stutters. "She knew your mom."

"Hello," she says.

I sit back down. "You look so much like her," I say.

Her eyes cut away from me, and Walter rubs her arm in a soothing gesture. "Why don't you go back in, and I'll be there in a minute," he tells her.

She nods her head and walks back to the house, then stops and looks at the door. She lifts it like it's nothing, leans it against the house, and walks inside.

"Now, do you have a phone?" he asks me.

I take the one out of my pocket. "They just issued me this one," I say, showing him.

He looks at it. "Do you have your own?" he asks. He's still staring at the phone, but his eyes keep drifting back towards the house.

"This is it. We weren't allowed to bring our own with us when they recruited us."

His eyes connect with mine, his face and voice serious. "You need to get a cheap one. One you buy yourself. A burner phone."

"Why?" I ask.

He taps the phone in my hand. "Because that one can be traced."

My stomach drops. I didn't even think about that. "Is that bad?" I ask. "If something happens, that means they could find me."

He rubs his chin. "Yes, they could. And they know where you are right now."

I drop the phone like it burned me.

"We're going to need to leave here soon. But keep this phone. If something does happen, they'll come help you. But if you want to come see us or anyone else, leave that phone behind. I'm going to run inside real quick, just wait a moment." He gets up and quickly walks to the house.

All I can do is stare at the phone. It's a blessing and a curse. But I didn't even think that me coming here would be a bad thing. Maybe if they see where I am, they'll think I'm visiting to tell them about Ania? But I'm surprised the phone hasn't rung. Maybe they aren't tracking it right now?

Walter comes back out of the house. When he gets to me he stays standing and hands me a scrap of paper. "Memorize this number. You'll be able to reach us at it. And if for any reason you need to hide, come and find us," he tells me.

Maybe he's being over cautious, especially because of what happened with Ania. But with all the kidnappings, maybe it's not too crazy.

I take the paper, along with my phone, and put them into my pocket. "I'll see you soon," I tell him, and it's a promise. Because I promised Ania that I would help Bronia any way I could.

"Be careful," he tells me.

I give him a small wave and close my eyes. I open them to find myself back in my room at headquarters. I sit down heavily on the bed and stare at the wall, unseeing and exhausted.

I don't even know how much time has passed when the phone in my pocket starts to ring. Is Mr. Smith calling me? No one else has the number. I pull it out and look at the screen.

Gregory.

FIVE

The phone sits in my palm; it keeps ringing with his name flashing on the screen. I'm so torn between talking with him, yelling at him, and ignoring his call altogether. But the curiosity of what he's going to say overrides everything else in my mind.

"Hello," I say after I finally decide to answer the call.

"Becca," he says my name on a rush of air.

I don't say anything. I don't even know how to have this conversation with him. I don't think he has any clue that I know about his power. I highly doubt Mr. Smith clued him in.

"Are you still there?" he asks.

I take a deep breath. "Yeah. I'm here," I say, and I know there's a lack of emotion in my voice. But I'm afraid if I let myself feel, this phone call is going to turn explosive.

"Are you okay?" If he was in front of me he would be wrapping me in his arms, and that almost hurts the most, because after everything, even in my anger, I'd probably welcome it.

But apparently my mouth has different plans. "You left me there," I tell him, the words rushing out. And I can see him, hanging out of the SUV as it speeds away. Leaving me alone.

Silence stretches out on the phone.

"I came back." His voice sounds tortured. "I jumped out of the car and ran back, but you were already gone. I didn't know where you went. I didn't know if they took you. It took our driver dragging me back to the SUV for me to leave."

I don't know how to respond to that, because even though I heard him yelling at the driver to stop, there's more to the situation that that. He's kept the secret that he can read minds from me. And even if he was ordered too, why wouldn't he tell me after he decided to break the rules to be with me?

"I can't do this right now," I tell him.

He breathes a heavy sigh into the phone. "All right. I'll see you tomorrow," he says, and I hang up without even saying goodbye.

I flop back on my bed and desperately try to clear my mind for a while. But it's not happening. Too many thoughts keep pinging around. What else is he hiding? Was he lying about his feelings for me? Could he be in league with Sariah? Maybe he has feelings for her?

I rub my temples. My thoughts are starting to sound like a conspiracy theorist's, and it's exhausting. I check the time on my phone—it's getting late. I doubt anyone is in the gym, and that's probably the only place capable of taking all my concentration right now.

I quickly change, then head out of my room and make all the crazy twists and turns to get to the gym. Thankfully, I actually get there. I guess I could have transported, especially since everyone saw me flicker, but they didn't see me actually transport. And I'm not sure if we need to keep that a secret still.

I walk over to the treadmill. I'd rather run outside, but I doubt that'd be allowed right now. And I have no desire to hunt down the indoor track. I set the speed and kick off at a fast pace, pushing my body hard so my mind will blank out.

My hopes of working out alone are quickly dashed with the opening of the gym door. Dexter pops his head inside, and a genuine smile spreads across my face. If it were anyone else, I would ignore them, but Dex is an awesome guy.

"Hey, Becca," he says when he spots me. I turn down the speed and hop off the treadmill so I can talk with him. I haven't seen him since shortly after we all arrived at headquarters.

"Hey Dex," I say, grateful it's him coming in here.

He walks over with his hands stuffed in the pockets of his workout shorts. "Hoping to work out alone?" I ask.

He shrugs and his cheeks turn a little red. "Yeah. Some of the other guys are kind of intense, so I like to come in at night when it's empty."

"How's it been going here?" I ask as he walks over to the weights.

He picks up some weights and racks a bar. I watch him sit down at the weight bench and my eyes widen at the number of pounds he put on the bar. There's no way he can bench press that. "I actually got to leave for two different trips," he tells me.

"Really? That's awesome. What for?" I ask, but my eyes haven't let the bar yet.

He lies down and adjusts his body so he's underneath it. "So my power has to do with minerals, rocks, gems, stuff like that. I went to a couple of mines to collect fresh samples."

He places his hands on the bar and pushes up to dislodge it. He slowly lowers the bar to his chest and then pushes it back up with hardly any difficulty. Well, who would have thought Dexter had it in him?

I wait to say anything until he racks the weights. "What do you do with the rocks?" I ask.

He does a few more reps and sits back up when he's done. "It's kind of hard to explain, but it's like my mind already knows what all these minerals can do. It's like being able to unlock all their potential, but that's the hard part. Because I need to take a mineral and make it more." He looks down and tilts his head back and forth like he's trying to decide something. He looks back up at me. "Want me to show you?" he asks.

Why not? I've got nothing better to do. "Lead the way, Dex."

We leave the gym and he takes me to the level below us and leads us to his laboratory. Dexter has his own laboratory. So many jokes could be made, but I resist...for now.

We walk in, and it's like walking into my chemistry class back at school. "What do you do in here?" I ask while I walk to a lab table and bend over to look through the microscope sitting there. I still don't know what I'm looking at half the time with these things.

"Have you ever heard of alchemy?" he asks, and I move my eyes from the microscope and look at his face closely. Yup, he's being completely serious.

"You mean when they tried to turn stuff into gold during medieval times?" I ask, because that's what they do in movies.

He waves off my comment as he fiddles with some test tubes. "It's so much more than that. The easiest way to explain it is when you take one substance and turn it into another. But I've been looking at taking a mineral and enhancing its properties. Like clear quartz is supposed to promote healing. But what if it *actually* healed you?"

That could change lives. "That would be amazing."

There are all sorts of people who think certain crystals have different healing or cleansing properties. I'm a little skeptical about all that, but if Dex has found out which rocks can do certain things—a thought pops into my head. I'm hesitant to ask him, but I've got to know. "Hey, any chance you can find a stone or crystal to block mind reading?" I ask, and as soon as the question is out, tension fills the room.

He hesitantly replaces the test tube he was inspecting and turns to face me fully. "Mind reading?" He asks the question slowly, like he needs to make sure he heard me correctly.

"Yeah," I say just as slowly, because that wasn't a specific question or anything. I really want to smack my own forehead right now.

He stares at me, probably waiting for more than my one-word answer, but I don't think I can tell him who. But maybe if a give him a little information without names? "There's someone here who can read minds. And I'd rather not have them do that with me."

He looks thoughtful for a moment and I hold my breath, waiting for his answer. "I'll look into it."

My body relaxes at his answer. "Thanks," I tell him.

The clock on the wall grabs my attention. I've got to get to bed and try to grab some sleep since I need to be up super early. "I better get going. I've got to leave in the morning. It was really good to see you," I tell Dex, and I'm being truthful with him.

"Mission?" he asks.

"Yeah," I say, and I'm hoping it's a recovery mission. But I won't let my hopes get too high.

"Tell Tony I said hi."

I do my best to school my features at his words, because only a few people know he's missing. I feel like more should know about what's going on, but Sariah was a new recruit. What if someone else who started with me is a traitor too? What if Dex says something to the wrong person about where we went?

But one thing I do know is that I really hope I can relay that message to Tony from Dexter, and soon.

SIX

"How come I only see you in this dream world?" I ask my mom. We're sitting on the rock pier at Meigs Point. I used to come to this beach with my grandparents, but never with my mom. The saltwater breeze dances across my skin. At least in this dream world it's warm, even though winter is quickly approaching.

"I don't know. I don't make the rules," she says.

Well, that answer kind of sucks.

I can feel her looking at me, but my eyes stay fixed on the horizon. Maybe someday it'll feel natural sitting next to her, but not yet.

"How's it going at headquarters?" she prods.

I let out a humorless laugh. "Besides the constant freak-outs I seem to have? Or how about my friend being kidnapped? But the best one, falling for a guy that knows every little thing that I think. How's that one?"

"Becca, it'd be no different for a soldier recently returning from war. Add in the fact that you're young and not trained for this, and sadly, I'm not surprised. This life you've been born into isn't going to be an easy one." Her voice makes her sound almost like a parent. Is this how our relationship would have been?

"I don't have the luxury right now to break down," I tell her, ignoring the comment about what I was born into. I think she could have prepared me more, and that'll probably always be a sore point with me, but maybe now she'll make up for it in these dreams.

"That's something that you might not be able to control. Sometimes these breakdowns will pop up out of nowhere," she tells me.

And I get it. This isn't something I can shrug off; it's not normal to experience all these things and act like it isn't affecting me. But I've got to figure out how to deal. Too many people are counting on me.

"You should go visit your grandpa again soon," she tells me.

Grandpa? That was out of left field. "Again with the cryptic suggestions?" I ask.

"I like to think of it as giving you a nudge."

"Any other 'nudges' you want to give me?" I ask, because I'll take whatever she's got to give.

She shakes her head, giving me a small smile, and stands up from our perch on the rocks. "Until we meet again," she says, lightly touching my shoulder, and walks away.

I stay on the rocks, kicking my feet as I watch her leave. Part of me thinks these dreams with my mom are only my subconscious trying to work things out, but another looks at all the crazy powers I've seen so far at Project Lightning and thinks anything is possible.

The waves below start to churn violently, the sky darkens, and lightning flashes in the distance above the water. Time to wake up.

I blink up at the ceiling, the alarm blaring near my head. I roll over, picking up my phone to turn off the alarm. I'd honestly rather throw it across the room. It's five am, and my body hates me right now. Plus these dreams are super draining. But I've got to get up and meet with Mr. Smith.

I head out for his office, but all I can think about is seeing Gregory. As soon as I'm near him he's going to know I know his secret. Can't really hide anything from a mind reader.

I knock on Mr. Smith's door, and he calls for me to enter.

"Morning, Becca," he says to me. It's just us. Mr. Rivers is nowhere to be seen. Old guy must need his sleep, and I'm jealous.

"You ready for today?" he asks me.

I sit in the seat in front of his desk. "We need to know what happened with Tony."

He nods. "Hopefully we'll get some answers real soon. And those answers will determine our next step."

"Am I meeting them at the last spot where we saw Tony?" I ask.

He pushes a button on his desk and a 3-D photo appears. "No. I'm going to have you meet Gregory here." He points at the picture and then pulls up an aerial photo and a map of the area. It's a dirt road with trees lining the sides, and I'm pretty sure it's the same road we traveled to drop Tony off. "It's close, but you'll wait there for Xavier and Raven. They should be there soon. We need to make sure the area is safe enough for all of you to proceed."

I study both photo and map. "Okay, I think I've got this," I tell him.

"Good. Do you have your phone on you?" he asks.

I pat my pocket. "Yup."

He leans towards me and puts his face level with mine. "Anything goes wrong, you get out of there. And if you have a problem transporting, call me right away."

"Got it," I tell him, and my stomach starts to twist into knots.

"Good luck," he says, and I take that as my cue to get going.

I close my eyes and think of the area, of where the map shows it, and what the picture looks like. I think of Gregory's face, because he'll be there. My body embraces the now present pull of transporting.

Before I even have a chance to open my eyes, I feel hands grab my shoulders.

Gregory's unique scent hits me like punch. I never knew betrayal had a scent. But I do now. And it's not disgusting—far from it, actually. Its clean laundry, Old Spice deodorant, and pure Gregory. Worst of all, the smell that used to make my heart lift now makes it clench in agony. I open my eyes to stare into his relieved green ones. He steps forward and pulls me into his chest.

For a quick moment I let him hold me, but I swiftly push myself out of his arms. He searches my face, probably my mind too, but I do my best to keep everything blank. I turn away, trying to block him in any way I can, and take in the surroundings. We're in the middle of nowhere. With jagged mountains in the distance. The cold air rushing off the mountain stings my cheeks. It's a beautiful place. And it's an isolated place.

His hand touches my arm, and I shake it off.

"I can't..." My voice trails off.

Enough with beating around the bush and trying to block him. *I know.*

His eyes widen a fraction, but he quickly recovers. And that pisses me off even more.

"You can't what?" he asks, still trying to save face and act like he doesn't know I'm talking to him in my mind.

I know.

My body is shaking, and my heart is hammering in my chest. It's like this *thing* is building inside, and at any moment this volcanic emotion is going to come bursting out. And everyone is going to get burned, including myself.

He flinches at the cutting words from my mind. His eyes look down and he runs his hands through his hair.

His silence is too much, and too late.

"I can't believe you!" The words erupt out of me. "I know what you can do. And every thought I've ever had around you, you knew. Nothing is secret, nothing is sacred. And I don't know if you were truthful with me or just told me things I wanted to hear." My chest is heaving and my hands keep clenching into fists.

"How?" he asks, his voice dull, not even bothering to try and deny any of my accusations.

"Ania told me. We were left at the bottom of that ramp with death only a few yards ahead. We had no idea what was going on with Tony. And she knew, she *knew* what your power is and couldn't understand why you didn't pick up on Tony's thoughts. And I had to watch her run for those soldiers, while I ran to you."

My voice breaks. "I ran to you, not knowing if I could trust you, but I hoped I still could. But you left me there."

He lets out a tortured moan and steps towards me. I hold up my hands and back away from him.

"I can't let you touch me right now," I tell him.

"How could you think I'd knowingly let Tony betray us? If he'd even thought anything like that, I would have pulled you guys out of there. I lost one of my best friends that day too." The heartbreaking emotion in his voice almost makes me back down, but this too important.

"How can you tell someone you love them and keep this kind of secret?" I ask him, and I'm doing my best to ignore his comment about Ania. I can't handle it; just talking about her sacrificing herself for me has me so close to another breakdown.

"I was ordered to," he tells me, his voice pleading for me to understand.

"You were ordered to stay away from me too, but you defied *that* one."

He rubs a hand over his face, and then he kicks out at the dirt, sending rocks flying. It's rare he shows himself losing control.

"Damn it, Becca. You have—" He's cut off by the sound of a car approaching.

This isn't the time anyways.

He turns away from the black sedan that just pulled up, and his gaze locks with mine. "We're not done talking about this," he says, and his words are a promise.

The car door opens and out steps Xavier, followed by Raven.

"We interrupting something?" Xavier asks slowly as he strides forward, his eyes going back and forth between us, brow raised.

Gregory completely ignores his question, his jaw firm. "Let's get in the cars and get to the spot."

He walks to another black car that I didn't notice before. He motions towards me, but there is no way I am getting in a car with him. I'm not ready for the fight that's brewing.

"I'll transport there," I say, and before anyone can object, I close my eyes and disappear.

SEVEN

Xavier, Raven, and Gregory stride towards me with purpose. I should have gotten in a car with them, because I've been pacing back and forth to stay warm. They better be able to use their powers to find out what went down here. We need to know what happened, and I can't even think about what Tony's going through right now. Any time I let a thought of him slip into my mind, it makes me sick to my stomach. And all I can think about is the large spot of dried blood.

Gregory's eyes sweep the area. "Show us what you found, Becca," he says, and it sounds like the car ride might have calmed him down.

He shoots me a tight smile. Then again, maybe it didn't.

I follow the trail to the cliff and walk over to where I found the blood. Thank goodness it hasn't rained. "The blood starts here, and the trail leads to the tire tracks over there." I point to a spot off in the distance.

Xavier pulls off his gloves as he walks forward and crouches down. Gregory steps up next to me and we both watch Xavier as his hand softly touches the earth. His eyes close and I watch him take deep breaths. I wonder what it's like. Is it like watching a movie in reverse? He rakes his fingers through the dirt and his facial muscles strain. His hands fist in the dirt and I take a step forward without thinking. To do what I'm not sure, but it looks like this is hurting him. "He's okay," Raven says softly. "Let him work."

After a few tense moments his eyes open, but they're unfocused and he doesn't say anything.

"I'm going to go talk with the animals," Raven says, and I kind of want to follow and see if she's like a Disney princess. But I'd probably scare off any animals and I don't want to distract her, especially if they know what happened with Tony. She walks by Xavier and softly caresses his shoulder as she passes by.

Xavier stays down in his crouched position for a while longer and I'm starting to get nervous, but he turns in our direction, his eyes still unfocused. "He was keeping watch when Sariah approached him. It completely surprised him, so he failed to notice the three guys that snuck up from behind."

I suck in a breath and grab Gregory's hand. His hand immediately tightens on mine.

"They quickly tackled him to the ground and put a gun to his head, forcing him up on his knees." I can picture the whole thing playing out, and it causes my heart to beat out of control. "Sariah started asking questions about the mission and about Becca. His silence bought him a beating."

The hair on the back of my neck stands up. Ania told me my mom was worried people would come for me. I don't get what the big deal is; so I can do more than my mom, it's not like I'm some all-powerful being. Why would they want me? Why take Tony? What are they hoping to gain from all of this? And does this have anything to do with the other agents that were kidnapped? There are way too many unanswered questions.

Xavier turns, his eyes locking with Gregory's. "I don't know if she needs to hear the rest." All the questions I just had floating around in my head stop at his words.

"Don't you dare try to shield me from this," I tell them, and I realize I'm still holding Gregory's hand and drop it quickly.

Gregory studies me closely. *Please, I need to hear*, I plead with him my mind. He nods his head for Xavier to continue.

Xavier takes a deep breath. "The beating was brutal. But the broken ribs weren't enough to break him." He pauses. "Neither was the gunshot to the thigh."

My breath stalls in my chest and my heart shatters. I reach up and fist hands into my hair.

"But that made him pass out. And that's when they dragged him to the van," Xavier tells us.

We hear crunching leaves and all of us turn to watch Raven walk back towards us. "The animals tell the same story. But they scattered at the gunshot. They kept saying something about an unnatural smell. I'm not sure what they meant by that though, maybe the vehicle," she says.

"Did you hear or see anything else?" Gregory asks Xavier.

Xavier stands to his full height and dusts off his hands. "The license plates were covered. But the passenger van they were driving looked like a newer model Hyundai. Sariah called one of the men Elliot. But I don't recognize any of them. I'm assuming they're hired men."

"Tony was still alive?" I ask Xavier.

He nods his head. "Yes. And that type of wound isn't fatal. He'll be down for a while, but he'll survive. They took him for a reason, so they'll treat his wounds."

That gives me a little comfort, but not much. I can't begin to imagine the pain he's in, or how scared he is. I hope he knows we're coming for him, that we'll find him.

"Why would they take him without leaving a note or demanding a ransom?" I ask, more to myself than anyone else.

"Maybe they haven't had time yet to make demands," Raven says.

I look down at the blood splatter still visible in the dirt. *Hang in there, Tony. We're going to find you.*

"Anything else?" Gregory asks, probably for our benefit, since he could literally pluck it from his mind.

"I'll check again, but I don't think so," Xavier says. He heads over to a spot next to the tire tracks.

"I think we're going to need to go and visit Sariah's family," Raven says as she adjusts the bright pink scarf around her neck.

"You're right," Gregory says. "I'm going to call Mr. Smith and fill him in. Let's see what the next move is. Because I highly doubt they're still anywhere in this part of Asia."

He walks away and I'm left standing awkwardly alone with Raven.

"So what do the animals—"

"Grenade! Run!" Xavier comes barreling towards us.

Raven turns and sprints away, but my legs won't move. I'm cemented to this spot.

Everything takes on a surreal feel, like I'm watching a movie of everyone rushing by, but I'm not really there. I can see Xavier waving his hands at me. And I can see the urgency on his face. But my vision blurs for a moment and I see the gate at the military compound. I hear Ania yelling in Polish.

"Becca! Transport now!" Gregory's scream pierces the horrendous memory that's trapped me.

I turn and stare at his face peeking from behind the car. "To me!" he yells.

My body responds on instinct at his command.

I blink and I'm tackling him to the ground.

He wraps his arms around me and flips us over, covering my body with his.

What about Xavier?

Gregory opens his mouth to answer, but a loud boom like multiple shotgun blasts pierces the air, cutting off any chance of him answering. And it's soon followed by a loud moan from Xavier.

Dirt and debris rain down on us, pelting our bodies. "Xavier?"

Gregory calls out once the debris settles, still holding me underneath him.

"I'm—" Loud, hacking coughs followed by a pained groan cuts off his words. "I'm okay," he finally manages to grunt out.

"Raven?" Gregory asks.

"Right behind you," she says. My eyes track her way and I can barely see her crouched down behind a car, her once baby-blue coat now covered in dirt.

Gregory takes a deep breath, pressing his body into mine. "Good," he says to himself. He unwinds his body from mine and stands. I lie still on the ground as he brushes himself off, his eyes scanning the scene. "What the hell was that?" he yells.

"I stopped looking after the van left. I didn't think they'd turn back around. But there was a trip wire planted for a grenade," Xavier says.

I hear the conversation continue around me, but I'm paralyzed on the ground. My arms and legs won't move. My heart won't stop racing, and the pressure in my chest is building, cutting off my air. My eyes track Gregory. Why can't he hear my screams?

A choking sound passes my lips. And his head snaps to mine.

Can't. Breathe.

He rushes towards me and drops to his knees. "Hey, look at me." His voice is calming.

Can't move.

"It's okay. Just focus on me. Don't look anywhere but my eyes," he tells me, and I can see him lightly touching my face, but I can't feel it. Why can't I feel it?

I look into his eyes. Hot tears streak down my face. *So weak.*

"No," he says, his voice firm. "You're so strong, baby. So strong. But we have to get you breathing slower or you're going to pass out. You're having a panic attack. I need you to try breathing in through your nose for ten beats, hold it, and then let it out slowly through your mouth. I'll do it with you."

I try. I try so hard, but the pressure on my chest won't ease.

"Keep going. You've got this."

"We've got incoming. Gregory, get her into the car," I hear Raven shout. "Xavier, you're going to have to help me get you in."

"What about the other car?" Xavier asks.

"Leave it," Gregory tells them. "They won't be able to trace anything, and I've worn gloves the whole time I've driven it."

He scoops me up in his arms and we're soon climbing into the back seat.

"The animals scattered at the explosion, but some of the birds came back and told me more humans are coming," Raven tells us.

The car starts and she whips around, peeling out of there. But my eyes don't leave Gregory's. "That's it, keep looking at me. Breathe with me."

I try, but it's hard bouncing around in the back seat. Gregory keeps looking at me and counting our breaths. Time feels odd, and I hear Raven and Xavier talking to someone who's yelling.

I keep trying to breathe with him. "There you go. Do you feel your chest loosening?" Gregory asks.

I focus on my lungs and I feel them relax a fraction.

"Good. That's good. Try moving your fingers and toes," Gregory says as his hand keeps stroking my hair.

I drop my eyes, but the grip on my forearm makes me snap them back to Gregory. "Keep those eyes on me. Okay?"

I nod my head. *I moved my head.*

"Yup. Now your fingers."

I clench my hands into fists and then slowly relax them. I do it five more times while still trying to breathe with Gregory.

"There you go. Do you want to try sitting up?" he asks.

I finally take stock of my body. I'm draped across his lap in the back seat.

"Yeah," I say, but it sounds more like a croak than an actual word, so I clear my throat a few times.

He lifts me off his body onto the seat next to him, but his hands don't leave me. He runs them up and down my arms. I look to the front of the car and see Xavier hunched forward.

"Xavier?" I ask, worried.

His face turns at my voice. His sleeve is torn, and he's got dirt covering his face and hair, blood covering his nose and mouth. "You okay?" he asks.

"Are *you* okay?" I ask instead.

The car takes a sharp corner, and Xavier lets out a grunt as he shifts a little in the seat. "Think I broke a rib, but I've had worse. I'm still here."

"I'm sorry," I say, choking on the words. He was almost blown to bits, and I'm back here only having a panic attack.

"Don't you say sorry," Gregory says, and I turn at the bite in his words. "You've endured more than anyone should have to in such a short amount of time. I don't know how you're still functioning," he says.

I know he means what he says, but I'm not ready to agree with him. "What happens now?" I ask, trying my best to change the subject.

He stares at me for a beat then exhales loudly. *Just drop it for now. Please.* He nods his head, and I'm so thankful he'll listen for now. "We need to head back to South Korea. But we've got to find a place to clean Xavier up first. They'll never let us in with him looking like that," Gregory says.

"How are you going to take care of him?" I ask.

"We've got a contact right over the border in Daeseong-dong," Raven tells us from the front seat, still steering us down the mountain. "But Mr. Smith called; he wants you to transport back to headquarters right away."

Why can't I just stay with you guys? I can't believe how easily I've fallen into talking to Gregory with my mind.

"You didn't enter this country with us, and you don't have the right paperwork," he says, sounding apologetic. "They might even have your picture from breaking into the compound or when you ran. No one can see you. It's too risky."

"Fine," I say.

"Oh, she said *fine*. It's never a good thing when a woman says *fine*," Xavier says from the front seat. He coughs and then groans. "Man, I hope this guy has some good painkillers."

"Are you sure you don't want me to stay and help?" I ask, watching Xavier try to shift in his seat.

"Raven and I have it covered. Get back to Mr. Smith," Gregory tells me.

I lay my head back against the seat and close my eyes. The car bumps over the uneven road. I picture Mr. Smith's office and keep my focus on that even as the car sways. I feel the air change around me, and when I open my eyes I'm back at headquarters and right in Mr. Smith's office.

EIGHT

Mr. Smith is sitting at his desk with his head in his hands when I transport into the room. I watch him unnoticed for a moment. He looks unsettled; he never looks like this. I clear my throat and he quickly sits up straight, his hands dropping to the top of his desk.

"Are you hurt?" he asks as he looks me over. I'm surprised that's the first thing he asks me.

"I'll be all right." At least physically it's only some small bruising. Emotionally, I'm a freaking mess.

We stare at each other for what feels like a lifetime. His face becomes a mask of steely determination. "We're going to figure this out, and we're getting Tony back," he tells me, his voice quiet but firm.

I try to swallow the emotion that wants to choke me. The guilt though, it's going to suffocate me. It's too much. I'm the reason he was taken. Xavier *just* got hurt because of this.

"Stop thinking," he commands me, like he knows my thoughts.

I look at him, but I can't get my mouth to form words.

"This is not your fault. And if you let your mind go down that road, you won't be any help in getting him back. I need you, but I can't have you broken." His words are harsh, but I get it. There will be a time to break, and it's inevitable I'll do it again. For now I've got to push those emotions down deep and desperately try to bury them. But it's kind of like being stuck in a round room, looking for a corner to cry in.

He watches me, like he knows what I'm trying to lock away.

Got it? his eyes seem to ask. I take a cleansing breath, and then I nod my head. It's a thin line between sanity and complete freak-out right now, but I'm clinging to my sanity with all I have.

"Good, because you're going to be infiltrating Sariah's house."

Okay, not what I expected, but it helps me snap myself out of it.

"Specifically her room. Search it. If there's a laptop, I want you to take it." He's no-nonsense right now.

A little B and E, because that's not against the law or anything. Then again, infiltrating a military compound in a foreign country wasn't child's play either.

"Hopefully something we find there can lead us to whoever's helping her, or places she might take Tony."

I'll do whatever it takes to get him back, even if it means breaking into her room. Tony would do it for me. He already took a bullet for me. I shake that thought away.

"How am I supposed to get in her room? The only places I've been able to transport to are ones I've either been to or that we have blueprints for."

Mr. Smith raises a brow.

"Don't tell me you've got blueprints." Cause that's a little creepy.

"They're public record," he says, like it's totally common to have. Does he keep blueprints of all our houses?

"Still kind of weird," I say quietly, needing to get that out there.

"Anyway." He shoots me a look clearly telling me to shut it. *Message received.* "Gregory, Raven, and Xavier will be en route to Concord, North Carolina by tomorrow."

"Why don't I just go there without them?" I ask.

"Because I need the other three to use their powers. We're going to have you meet them here, at the former Stonewall Jackson Training School." He types something on his desk and a 3-D image pops up showing photos of the place.

I lean closer and look at the pictures. Some of the buildings had been covered in ivy. Not in that cool historic way, but in the way of nature reclaiming an area where something bad happened. Plus, even just looking at the photos, the place has the feeling of desolation about it. Like evil things took place there. "Next time can you guys pick a place that looks less like a horror film set?" I ask, because it does.

I look closely at the caption of one of the photos. "Does that say it's a reform school for delinquent boys? Everyone knows that's like code for kids getting tortured."

He waves away the disgust in my voice, like it's no big deal. The place is probably the perfect setting for a horror movie, or one of the shows about ghost hunting. I should look that up later; I bet there's already an episode out there about it.

"It's closed now," he says, like that changes anything.

I lean back in the chair and cross my arms over my chest. "Probably because people got tired of being haunted by the ghosts of tortured teen boys."

"Becca," he says my name like a plea.

I just shrug. They probably did.

"You won't meet up with the others for two days, and we'll go over the blueprints for Sariah's house then. It'll take them a bit to get back here.

"Also, next time, try transporting on the other side of my office door," he says, and his eyes look down and focus on the task of organizing the papers on his cluttered desk.

"Why?" I ask, causing him to look back up.

"Do you want me walking into your bedroom unannounced?" he asks, his brows raised.

Yeah, that'd be weird. "Good point."

"Get out of here." His last words are an order, not a suggestion.

I walk out of his office and head straight to my room. I'm in desperate need of a shower and maybe sleep, because my body feels wasted. But the fear of whatever nightmares are lurking behind my eyes makes me want to rethink the sleep part.

———————

MY CELL RINGS as I walk out of the bathroom. Steam trails me from the long shower I just took. I reach my bed and grab the phone as it goes off again. Gregory's name flashes on the screen. My finger hovers over the decline button, but my heart tugs at me. I drop onto my bed.

I tap accept.

"Hello," I say.

A long, relieved sigh is breathed into the phone. "Becca." He says my name like a plea. Like he's begging for something only I can give him.

His voice makes my chin drop to my chest with the weight of the ever-pressing stress weighing on me. "How's Xavier doing?" I ask, trying to keep control of wherever this conversation might head.

"He's on some pretty good pain pills and he's icing his ribs, but he's okay," he tells me. He sounds tired, compliant.

"Good. Did he tell you more about what he saw before the land-mine exploded?" I ask, glad he's letting me steer this conversation.

"Yeah, the van stopped a bit down the road and one of the guys came back to set the trap. I'm guessing someone knew about Xavier's power. It's why they didn't set it when everyone was still there." This complicates things.

"It makes sense. If they know about Tony and Xavier, they probably know what everyone can do."

He makes a sound of agreement, and then it's just silence for a bit.

"Come see me." The words rush out of him. "Our flight isn't until tomorrow. I just...let me explain some more. Let me make sure you're okay. Please."

How much longer am I going to put this off? I don't even know what's going to happen with us, but I know that I'm going to have to work with him. Probably for years. And with everything that happened with Tony, and what transpired today, we've got to figure out how to work with one another. There are so many emotions swimming through me, and I don't want the anger to weigh me down anymore.

"Where are you?" I ask, my voice lacking any strength, just resigned.

"At the InterContinental Alpensia Resort in Pyeongchang." He talks fast and sounds somewhat excited. I'm not sure why, because this is probably going to be awkward at best. "I'll text you the address so you can pull it up on a map. And I've got the blueprints of the hotel so you can just transport to my room."

"Pyeongchang?" I know I just butchered the city's name.

"We stayed in South Korea." They didn't get that far. I'm surprised they didn't try to get to Japan.

"All right. I'll see you soon," I tell him.

"Thank you," he says.

"For what?" I ask.

"For being willing to talk with me," he says sincerely.

I take the phone from my ear and stare at it for a moment, and then I end the call.

My phone vibrates soon after I hang up, and I pull up the text from him. I plug the address in and look at the satellite image. I stare at it for a few moments and then look at the blueprints he sent me, still having that internal debate, but it feels right to go to him. I'm trusting my gut on this one.

I pull some clothes on and quickly braid my hair. I pick up the phone and look at everything once more. then I close my eyes and feel the pull of my body leaving my bed. I feel the air shift around me. When I open them he's there, sitting on his own bed with his head down and his hands clasped between his legs. His whole body seems slumped in exhaustion.

His head snaps up.

"Heard me?" I ask, and now I want to kick myself for how harsh my voice sounds, considering I just agreed to come here and hear him out. I guess I'm still a lot angrier than I thought, even if he just helped me out with my panic attack.

He lifts his hands in a helpless gesture.

This was a mistake. I shouldn't have come.

He stands up quickly and backs me into the door until his arms cage me in. I'm this close to baring my teeth at him. "Stay," he orders, his voice choked with emotion.

He drops his head for a moment, putting himself closer to my body. His presence almost overwhelms me, because part of me wants to feel his body press against mine, but I also kind of want to kick him in the balls. Two extremely different reactions, but whatever. He looks back up. "Just listen to me for a moment." He struggles to get the words out.

I take a deep breath, praying for patience. He waits, letting me calm down a bit.

"Do you have any idea what it's like to be a kid and hear *everything* that people are thinking? Do you want to know the sick and twisted things I've heard in people's minds?"

I can't even image the things he's heard.

He leans his face closer to mine. "Can you guess how many times I hid in my grandparents' basement just to get away from the constant noise?" His face looks drawn and haunted.

"I thought about taking my own life numerous times. No nine-year-old should want to do that."

Tears burn at the back of my eyes at the utter anguish I hear in his voice. And my heart aches for the lonely boy he was.

"I had no one to help me. There's something cruel about feeling utterly alone when your mind is filled with multiple voices. I was going crazy until Mr. Smith found me. I honestly thought they were going to throw me into a padded room."

He lifts his hands off the door and frames my face. "But being with you calmed my soul in a way I haven't felt since my parents were still alive."

I try to swallow the emotions that are starting to suffocate me.

"Can you imagine what it was like to try to have friends, or even date?"

Okay, I really don't want to hear about other girls, but I can't image going through school without friends or being around the person I had a crush on.

He lifts his hands in a helpless gesture. "Sorry. I'm only bringing it up because I haven't dated."

My mouth drops open, but I quickly close it with a snap.

I swiftly clear away the thoughts of possibly being his first kiss and focus back on the matter at hand. "I don't know if I'll ever get used to this," I admit. "And to be honest, I don't think I want to. I don't want you to always know what I'm thinking. I want to share everything with you, but only when I feel comfortable doing it. I still need to have my own thoughts."

"I know, but you haven't given me the chance yet to tell you that this is something we can work on."

"What?" My voice rises to an extremely unattractive octave.

He lifts a hand back to my face and strokes my temple with his thumb, causing my body to relax but my senses to heighten. "Ania and I spent a lot of time together, so we decided to try to find a way to shield her thoughts from me."

This is new.

"Distance works, obviously, but something I have to work on is tuning you out, and you need to work on being aware of me. For some reason, I hear you the most clearly out of anyone."

Awesome. "What exactly do you hear?" I ask, because there's always so much going on in my mind.

He tilts his head to side. "Sometimes I hear clear sentences. Like if you and I are just having a conversation. Other times it's snippets of a thought. Almost like I can hear any word you think."

"So you're saying my thoughts are a lot clearer and broadcasted than anyone else's?"

He nods his head as he takes a piece of my hair between his fingers, lightly rubbing it.

"That sucks," I tell him.

He laughs slowly. "I know, but we'll figure it out. Hopefully together?"

His words are basically begging me to forgive and move on, but with him. Am I ready to do that? Am I ready to push aside the fact that after he broke Mr. Smith's command not to get involved with me, he didn't tell me his power?

"It wasn't exactly the best time to tell you. We were preparing for a mission. You were almost kidnapped at the cabin. I wasn't thinking I had to tell you then. I figured after we got back from North Korea I'd have the chance to tell you everything. But the whole mission went to hell, and here we are now."

I scowl up at the ceiling; this is what I'm talking about when I said I wanted my thoughts to be my own. But even though he can read those questions, he's not getting what has made me so angry. "You know there's never a right time. You just do it. I would have been mad either way, but if *you* had told me, it wouldn't have lasted as long. And we could have worked this out faster."

"Does this mean there's still a 'we'?" he asks.

"I mean, I'm still kind of mad, but I get it," I tell him, and I do. Do I wish he had told me? Yes. Am I trying to understand? Yes. Am I worried that there are other things he's hiding for me? Of course. And I'm still embarrassed about all the thoughts I've had about him, and I'm still kind of pissed about that.

"We'll work on this," he promises me.

Well, I probably have a faster solution than he does. "I think I might have found a solution. But it's not a hundred percent yet." I don't bother thinking before telling him this. Because he'll just pick it up anyways.

"Remember Dexter?" I ask.

He nods slowly, so I tell him all about the conversation we had, and Dexter's promise to look into a stone.

"Did you tell him about me?" he asks hesitantly.

"No. But it won't take a genius to figure it out; it's from a short list of people." I mean really, there are only so many people at Project Lightning, and only so many we know.

"It's okay, he would have probably found out eventually."

We stand there staring at each other in silence. Lots of words still left unsaid. But a lot more to things to come between us...if we let it.

His fingers trail up my arm and then he lightly clasps my chin. "I need you to know I'm sorry."

"I know." And I do know he's sorry. I can feel it in how he looks at me, like I'm the most important person in the world to him. And in the way his body always seems to take a protective stance around me, like he'll always shield me if he can. Most of all, my heart knows, even if my brain is questioning everything.

"Forgive me?" he asks.

"I'm getting there," I tell him honestly. Because even though he's the only guy that's made my heart skip a beat, he's also the only one who's made it crack in two.

"I'll take whatever you'll give me." He steps away from me, the warmth leaving with him. Part of me was hoping he would lean in and kiss me. Stupid hormones. But the part that needs space is stronger, and I'm glad he recognizes that better than me.

He bites his lips and hesitates, and I've got a feeling I'm not going to like what comes out of his mouth next. "How are you doing from earlier?" he asks me.

"Fine," is my automatic reply.

He raises a brow at my response, causing me to huff out a breath. Might as well tell him since he'll just pick up my thoughts anyway.

"No seventeen-year-old should almost be blown up twice in a week's time," I say, my voice breaking a little on the words.

"You're right," he says, but I'm not listening to him. Because now that I've said these words out loud, it's making me lost in them, like they need to spill out.

"No seventeen-year-old should watch her friend die. Or jump at loud noises. Or be afraid to go to sleep because of the memories that linger, infecting her dreams." Tears stream down my face.

"Becca."

I ignore how my name sounds so tender on his lips and finish venting. "And I know we're not *normal*. But is this what life is going to be like from now on? One near-death experience to the next? I didn't ask for any of this. I was born into this. And I agreed to come here in order to make a difference. But I can't make a difference if I'm dead or hiding under my covers."

He looks like he wants to hug me, but thankfully he lets me pull myself together. For a few minutes I take huge breaths and let them out slowly, just like he showed me in the car.

I look at a spot over his shoulder. "So, uh, Sariah's place?" I ask in a desperate attempt to change the subject.

Out of the corner of my eye I watch him rock back on his heels, hands slipping into his pockets. "Yeah. Hopefully we'll find something there," he says, thankfully going along with my need to take the focus off of me.

"How did you not pick up anything from her?" I ask the question that I didn't even know has been bugging me.

"We were hardly at headquarters since you got recruited. And anytime I was focusing on her, her thoughts were always angry. They were focused on you a lot. I assumed it was just jealousy. But I never even caught a glimpse of her plotting to do anything she's done."

"But what about when she was at her interview?" I ask.

His whole body stills. "I wasn't there," he says the words slowly, like he just realized something, and it's left a bad taste in his mouth.

"Aren't you usually?" I ask, confused.

"Yes," he says, and drags a hand over his mouth.

"Why do you think that was?" I ask him, a sick feeling growing in the pit of my stomach.

"I think I was kept away from her interview on purpose. And with the way the grenade was planted where we last saw Tony... someone who knows about what we were doing, where we are, and what all our powers are must be helping her. They're playing our own powers against us. Someone at Project Lightning is helping her."

"We've got a traitor," I say, and he nods his head.

NINE

Traitor. The word alone terrifies me and makes me sick.

"What do we do?" I ask.

"*We're* not going to do anything. As soon as you leave, I'm going to call Mr. Smith."

I rub a hand over my face, then into my hair where I grip it at the roots. Gregory gently removes it and links his finger with mine.

"Mr. Smith *will* get to the bottom of this and we'll do whatever needs to be done," he says.

He's right. I know it. Just like I know Mr. Smith will take whatever measures he needs to. I look over Gregory's shoulder and my eyes catch on the clock on the nightstand.

"You should get back anyways so I can call him," he says.

"Yeah. I think I need sleep."

He nods and starts to lift his arms like he's going to embrace me, but my body jerks back a bit, dropping his hand that's still linked with mine. He takes a step back, and I'm grateful because I'm not ready for that yet. "I'll take care of it. You go and relax," he tells me, trying to cover his sadness and failing miserably.

I close my eyes so I won't have to see the rejection written across his face, and at the last second think of the only place that I can imagine relaxing right now.

The familiar smell of Grandpa's office washes over me, and all the tension my body's been holding seems to melt away. I hear his and Grandma's voices coming through the crack in the door, along with the clink of silverware. I look at the clock; they're probably just finishing lunch. It's been so long since I've seen Grandma, but she doesn't know about what my power is. And I have a feeling if she saw me walk in without hearing the front door, it would give her heart failure. Grandpa will be coming in soon for his daily ritual of reading the newspaper, even though I told him he can just do it on his phone. Old habits die hard and all that, but some sort of normalcy right now is a nice thought.

I sink down into one of the armchairs that sits in the corner of the room. The sound of clinking plates and utensils lulls me a bit. I'll just close my eyes for a bit; he'll be in soon.

A warm hand brushes the hair off my forehead. My eyes slowly open, and Grandpa's smiling face looks back at me. But the longer he stares, the more concerned his eyes grow.

"What is it?" he asks, really searching my face. I've never been really good at hiding my feelings from him.

"Bad day." I try to say the words with strength, but they come out a little broken. My hands start to shake and my heart rate picks up.

He pulls me into his arms, encasing me in his warmth and familiar scent of cloves mixed with leather. "Take a deep breath," he says, coaching me.

I do as he says, and the tightness in my chest begins to lessen. "Your dad used to come to me after bad missions and deployments," he says as he runs his hand up and down my back.

I stay silent, afraid to let my voice be what pulls him out of whatever memory he's reliving about my dad, because he hardly ever talks about him. So I force myself to calm down, staying in his arms, hoping he'll keep going.

"After Desert Storm there was still a lot of activity going on in

Iraq, and your dad took part in some of those operations. He came home from one and he had this haunted sadness about him. He would be looking at me, but his eyes were lost. It took him a bit to get the words out, but they had just dropped bombs on several targets and a lot of Iraqi soldiers died that day.

"He told me that no matter how much they were working towards the greater good, it never got easier knowing he was part of the reason a wife was being told her husband wasn't coming home. That a mother would be crying over an unmarked grave. That friends would be split up, and some of the unfortunate ones would live with the memories of the dying crying out in agony. Even after he started working for Mr. Smith, he'd get that haunted look in his eyes when he would tell me some of things he had to do."

Is this the future I'm going to have? Is this the reason my mom turned to drugs? To numb herself from reliving the memories of the things she'd seen and done?

"When he met your mother, that look changed. He'd found someone who understood exactly what he felt. He didn't pretend with her. In each other they found peace. I only wish it had been for a longer amount of time. Because I think in you they would have found hope. And hope is a powerful thing. It's that flicker of light when you're sure everything has been snuffed out. It's a chance when everything else has failed you."

His words are like an arrow straight to my heart, piercing a pain that had started to dull. I know he doesn't see that, that he's probably hoping to give me some sort of solace. But it's hard to talk about one of the most important men in my life that I never even got a chance to meet.

I stay in his arms, soaking up the warmth he's offering. So grateful I have him, that my dad had him.

"Aren't you worried that they know Dad told you all this stuff?" I ask, my head still resting against his shoulder.

He shakes his head, his stubble scratching my chin. "No, I'm like a vault. Your dad knew he could tell me anything. The same goes for you."

I squeeze my arms tight around him, bracing him for my words to come. "Today was the second time in a couple days where I was running from an explosion."

His whole body stiffens, and I'm pretty sure he just whispered, "Damn it."

"I'm pulling you out," he tells me quickly.

I pull back from him so he can see the determination on my face. "No, Grandpa."

His hands move up to the top of my arms and he grips them. "You're seventeen. I never thought you'd be facing this kind of stuff now. Later on, yes, but not right off the bat."

I don't disagree with him, but there's something he hasn't taken into consideration. "They need my power."

"Yes, but—"

"Grandpa, they need me now more than ever. Someone's kidnapping the children of Project Lightning agents. I'm going to help find them, and I need to help find Tony too."

He lets me go to rub a hand over this face, and then he looks into my eyes, a sad smile on his lips. He nods his head like he's answered his own question in his mind. "You're so determined. Just like your dad."

"Is that such a bad thing?" I ask.

He huffs out a humorless laugh. "Wait till you have kids one day. I'll remind you of this conversation."

If I live long enough to have kids. But I won't say that thought out loud; it'll only upset him.

We stare at each other in silence until he straightens up and looks towards his office door. "Well, how about we go see Grandma?" he asks, trying hard to lighten the heaviness in the room.

"Is she going to freak out about me just appearing?" I ask.

He shrugs. "Hopefully she'll just be so excited to see you that she'll forget to ask."

I climb out of the chair and my body protests at the movement. I must have slept for almost an hour. At least I didn't dream.

We walk out of the office and head towards the kitchen.

"Joe, I was thinking we'd go to the store—" Grandma starts saying, but as soon as her eyes land on me she freezes.

"Becca," she says, her voice a whisper.

"Hey, Grandma," I say, giving a little wave. I can't tell if she's happy about seeing me or not.

She beams at me and opens her arms. I walk quickly over to her and into them. The smell of her Chanel perfume fills my nose and calms some of the panic that keeps coursing through me. "What are you doing here?" she asks.

"I missed you guys." And man have I missed them. I miss the life I had. A year ago I was playing basketball, thinking about college scholarships, running errands with them on the weekends. But now... I never thought this would be my life.

She pulls back from our hug. Some emotion passes through her eyes, but I'm not quite sure what it is. "How long do we have you for?" she asks.

"Just a little bit."

Her displeasure flashes across her face, but she quickly schools her features. "Come sit. Let's get you something to eat. You look like you've lost weight."

Is it a universal thing for grandmas to want to feed you? I'm pretty sure there's a handbook somewhere and it says that.

"Sure, Grandma." After all, I haven't eaten a real meal in a while.

She bustles around the kitchen until a plate of waffles and fruit is set in front of me. "Leftovers from breakfast," she tells me, almost embarrassed.

It looks like heaven to me. I dig in while they both sit at the table with me.

"How you doing?" she asks me.

I take a swig of juice, using that moment to think of an answer that won't scare her. I may be able to tell Grandpa things, but she'd never be able to handle it. "Missing home, but I'm fine. Just busy," I say, and try to give her my most convincing smile.

"Will you be back for Thanksgiving?" she asks me.

I haven't even thought about the holidays. "I don't know," I tell her in all honesty.

She wipes invisible crumbs off the table, her stare avoiding mine.

"I'd like to, but there's a lot going on," I tell her, hoping that answer will mollify her.

She looks me straight in the eye. "Well, I'll expect you at Christmas. No excuses."

I look at Grandpa. "When did she get so pushy?" I ask.

He laughs. "When you left. Don't think she knows what to do with herself now."

"Oh, hush," she says. "You're never too old to change."

My brows shoot up at that, and I'm glad I don't have a mouthful of food right now or Grandpa would be preforming the Heimlich.

I finish my plate and then look at the clock. I need to go. I've been here a while, but I also need more sleep than what I got in Grandpa's office. "Sorry, Grandma, but I've got to head out."

Her forehead wrinkles. "So soon? Do you want to pack some food for the car ride back?" she asks as she walks over to the pantry next to the kitchen sink. "Is there a car out front waiting?" She pulls back the curtain over the sink, looking out at the street.

"Uh, no."

She looks from me to Grandpa, and then back to the window. Guess this is the best time for her to see what I can do. "Here, it'll be easier for me to show you than explain," I tell her.

I wait for her eyes to lock with mine. As soon as I see them focus on me, I maintain that eye contact. In the time it takes for her to blink, I'm already behind her and tapping her on the shoulder.

She whips around. One of her hands flies to her chest and the other grabs the edge of the counter. "How?" she asks.

I give her a small smile. "That's my power. I can transport anywhere."

I watch her visibly swallow and school her features, hiding whatever else she's thinking. Kind of wish Gregory was here to tell me what's going through her mind. She stands taller, smoothing out invisible creases in her blouse. "Well, then that definitely means you can make it home for Christmas."

A sharp bark of laughter escapes me, catching us all off guard. But it also makes my heart a little lighter to truly laugh at something. That's not what I thought she'd say. "Okay, Grandma."

Grandpa joins the two us by the counter. I hug Grandma first. It's a quick hug like earlier. But as she releases me, I'm quickly swept up into Grandpa's embrace. One of his hands strokes my hair while the other holds me tightly. "Any time you need me, just come home and I'll be here," he says in a soft voice into my hair. "You are never alone. You don't have to face all these trials by yourself."

I take a deep breath to try to ease the tears that desperately want to form.

"I love you, sweets. Don't forget that," he tells me.

"I love you too, Grandpa," I tell him, my voice little more than a whisper.

"You make me so proud. And I know your dad is proud of you too." With those words, the dam breaks and tears stream down my face. What is with all the crying lately? But I don't want him to see them, so I quickly step out of his arms, close my eyes, and transport back to my room at headquarters.

I drop onto my bed and let my tears soak my pillow. I don't know if my dad would be proud of me, but hopefully he will be soon.

TEN

"They're going to be coming for you."

Not this cryptic crap again. "You going to give me more than that?" I ask.

"Are you always this fresh?" my mom asks.

It's on the tip of my tongue to comment that she would know the answer to that question if she had been around me growing up. But instead my shoulders slump and I look to our surroundings to ground myself in this dream instead of lashing out. It's not her I'm mad at. Well, that's not true; I'm still kind of mad at her. But right now I'm frustrated and she's getting the brunt of it.

We're standing on the edge of a cliff this time. The air is briny and thick. Angry waves break on the rocks below. The sound is almost deafening, but I heard her talking to me just fine. I wonder if she picks the locations of these "dream meetings" or if this is all my subconscious. It does kind of match my mood.

"Who's coming?" I ask, my tone more sincere this time. It also sounds tired. The sky above us darkens a bit, like it's reflecting what I'm feeling inside.

She closes her eyes, like she's seeing something in her mind. She slowly opens them and her gaze pierces mine. "Your dad gave you so much more than I did. And they'll know that too."

I wait for more. But that just leads to me awkwardly standing here on these flat grey rocks, not getting anything else. "Come on. Just a little bit more info?" I've got no shame that I'm begging her.

"You know it doesn't work that way," she says, sounding almost apologetic.

"Well, why not?" I turn my back to the waves, giving her all my attention.

She throws her hands up into the air. "I don't make the rules."

"There are rules here?" Because that's new to me. Doesn't it kind of break all sorts of rules that she comes to me in my dreams in the first place?

"Of course there are. There always are."

I want to prod her about that, but it's pointless, so I motion with my hand for her to keep going.

"If I tell you too much, they won't let me come see you anymore. I won't get to warn you at all."

"Who's they?" I ask, using air quotes for "they," because these dreams are like a bad movie.

She gives me a pointed look.

I roll my eyes. "Fine, just another thing you can't say."

The sound of the waves below gets louder and I look down and see them getting larger. I look back at my mom, and she begins to say something, but I cut her off. "Let me guess. You've got to go." Her mouth pulls into a frown. "The dream starts to get more violent when you're about to leave."

She looks around like it's the first time she's noticed it. "I guess you're right. Well anyways, I'm sure I'll see you soon."

"Catch you later."

She shakes her head at me and then walks away, leaving me at the cliff alone.

It's actually kind of peaceful here. The violent sound of the waves *below helps distract me from my thoughts, but I know I won't get to stay for long.*

Lightning shoots across the inky sky, and that's my cue to leave.

The sound of rapid knocking on my door wakes me.

I roll out of bed and amble towards it. The knocking starts again. *Geez, someone seriously needs to learn patience.*

I throw open the door, ready to let whoever it is know how rude they're being, but I'm greeted by the faces of Mr. Smith and Mr. Rivers. I immediately stand a little straighter and run my fingers through my hair. I know I'm rocking some awful bedhead right now.

"Did we wake you?" Mr. Rivers asks. His eyes keep scrutinizing my disheveled clothes and hair.

"It's fine," I say, trying to smooth out my clothes that I've slept in the last several hours. Probably should have changed before I passed out, but I was too tired to care.

"May we come in?" Mr. Smith asks, angling his body to come in whether I wanted them to or not.

"Uh, of course." I step back and allow them to enter my room. Thankfully I haven't been here much, so I don't have any underwear hanging anywhere. Mr. Rivers ambles over to the desk chair in my room and slowly lowers himself into it, while Mr. Smith stands, taking up the center of the room.

I follow them in and stand against the wall. I cross my arms and then uncross them. I've got no clue what they're here for.

"Sit," Mr. Rivers says in his raspy voice, and without hesitation, I do.

My heart races as I stare at Mr. Rivers. My nerves are making me feel all over the place.

"Where were you earlier?" Mr. Rivers asks, and his voice is calm, almost gently questioning.

"I've been sleeping," I answer, completely confused as to what he's trying to get at.

He looks at Mr. Smith with a *you try* expression.

"Becca," Mr. Smith says on a sigh. "Where did you go after you left my office?"

My phone. They must have tracked it. I don't want to tell him I was with Gregory, even though he might already know I was there, but maybe if he asks about that later I can say we were talking about the mission. Which technically we were. But I'd rather not delve into the visit with Gregory, and since his power means I can't lie to him, I've got to find a loophole.

"Answer him," Mr. Rivers says in an oddly calm voice, all trace of rasp gone, interrupting my thoughts.

"At my grandparents'." The words tumble out of me. But this is okay, I can work with this.

"Why?" Mr. Smith asks.

"Because I miss them," I tell him without hesitation.

"Did you tell—" He's cut off by the ringing on a cell phone, and I have never wanted to kiss a phone before.

Mr. Smith pulls it out of his pocket and stares at it for a moment before answering. "Smith," he says into the phone.

Mr. Rivers stares at me a moment longer like he's trying to figure me out, but then he gives his head a minute shake and focuses on Mr. Smith.

Mr. Smith doesn't say anything to whoever is talking to him, but tension rolls off him, causing it to ratchet up in the room. It coils around me, suffocating. This is a bad call. "I'll take care of it," Mr. Smith says evenly, and puts the phone back in his pocket.

He looks between Mr. Rivers and me. "Another child was kidnapped from her home just now."

My stomach sinks. Nothing we've done has helped this situation. "Gregory, Xavier, and Raven are currently headed back here. They're going to have to make a detour," Mr. Smith says, but his words are directed at Mr. Rivers.

"Are you going to send the girl?" Mr. Rivers asks.

"Yes. We need someone there sooner since Xavier is too far," Mr. Smith tells him.

I'm assuming they're talking about me. But do they really need to act like I'm not standing here?

Mr. Smith looks at me. "I'm going to need you to transport to the house of another agent."

"All right." I'm totally on board with doing this. We've got to find these kids. Bronia's face pops into the forefront of my mind. What if they find her and take her too? Maybe I should call Walter. But he said to call from a different phone, and they might have left already anyway.

Mr. Rivers slowly rises from the desk chair with the help of his cane.

"Meet me in my office in ten minutes," Mr. Smith tells me. "I'm going to pull up satellite photos and coordinates. And we'll finish this conversation about where you were later."

"Yes, sir." The words totally slip out, but apparently they seem to please him, because a slight smirk pulls at his mouth before his lips set back in a firm line.

Both men head for the door, but before they exit, Mr. Rivers stops and looks at me. "You're only to go where Mr. Smith tells you to. And you call him with any important information. Do you understand?" he asks while he gently pats my arm.

A strange burning sensation rushes down my arms, but I shake it off. Probably just nerves. "Yes," I answer.

They leave the room and I hurry into the bathroom to get ready to leave.

I KNOCK on Mr. Smith's door and wait for a response. The door opens and Chelsea stands to the side to let me in. She doesn't say anything, but the only time I've heard her talk is when she showed up at my room.

"Thank you for being quick, Becca," Mr. Smith says to me, occupied with something on his desk. Mr. Rivers looks over at me from his seat in front of the desk, and Chelsea takes a spot standing against the wall. And I'm just here all awkward in the middle of the room.

Mr. Smith looks up at me and settles his hands on the desk in front of him. "I'm going to send you to Portsmouth, England. To an area called Southsea. It's right near a large port in southern England. In a minute we're going to video conference with Robert. His daughter Poppy has been kidnapped."

My chest feels tight. How am I going to help this guy? What can I do? I mean, I've watched some episodes of *Criminal Minds*, but I don't think that counts for anything. Who they really need is Xavier.

Mr. Smith leans forward, forcing my attention. "This just happened. I need eyes immediately. Robert is trying so hard to help, but it's challenging when you're so intimately involved. It'll probably be a couple of hours before more help can arrive.

"Look around and try to find anything he's missed. Or maybe something he hasn't thought of. The first few hours are crucial. Call me right away if you find something."

"Okay." I know my voice betrays me and doesn't sound okay at all.

"You'll do fine," Mr. River says, and it's the first time I've ever heard him sound grandfatherly; he usually just looks the part in those sweater vests. But his words provide comfort.

"Maybe this will help in finding Tony," Mr. Smith says.

Man, I hope so.

Mr. Smith presses some buttons on his desk and a holographic image pops up. It's a man in his thirties. His blonde hair is a mess, but not in an intentional way, and his square face is set in a hard line. He looks as if someone says one wrong word and he'll snap. Don't really blame him though.

"Robert, this is Rebecca Hunter," Mr. Smith says, motioning towards me. "She'll be transporting into your home here in a just a moment. She's going to start helping right away. The rest of the team will be there in a couple of hours."

"Yes, sir," Robert says, his voice rough and thick with an English accent. They must have briefed him about what my power was beforehand.

Mr. Smith looks back up at me. "You ready?" he asks.

I nod.

"Good. Here's the satellite image of the street." He presses another button and an image appears. "Robert, I'm going to zoom out on you so she can see the room."

The room Robert's in comes into focus. It's your typical family room, with a few toys scattered on the ground behind him. I'm guessing he's sitting at a table. I focus on the view of the street on the map, and study the room one more time. I focus on the spot behind him, next to the coffee table. "See you in a second," I tell Robert.

I close my eyes and keep the image in my mind. I feel the tug on my body and I open my eyes.

Robert's still sitting in front of his computer at a kitchen table when I transport into the room next to him.

"Blimey!" he shouts. Huh, didn't know anyone actually said that word. But he does apparently, along with some other curses. Half of them I've never heard before.

"Sorry. It always shocks people the first time," I tell him.

"Becca," Mr. Smith says from the computer screen. Both of us turn to look at him. "See how you can help. The rest of the team won't be there until tomorrow. Robert, we'll be in contact. We're pulling surveillance videos now. We'll find her." His words are a vow.

Robert closes out the video and allows his body to slump, but only for a moment. He rubs a hand over his reddish beard and then straightens up in his seat. "Not sure how you're going to help," he says as he turns towards me. His brown eyes seem wary. And I know he's looking at me like *What can a seventeen-year-old girl do*, but I just want to help in any way I can.

"Maybe there's something you haven't thought of?" I'm so out of my depth here.

"What do you know?" he asks, watching me closely.

"Not much. Just that your daughter Poppy was taken." His whole body seems to tense when I say her name. "Maybe you can tell me?" I ask.

He gets up from his seat. He towers over me, not only in height, but the sheer size of him. Guy has got muscles for days. He walks over to the fireplace and looks at the photos on the mantel. I step up beside him and see numerous pictures of a seven-year-old girl with golden curls and the biggest smile I've ever seen.

"She's beautiful," I tell him, my voice quiet.

"She is." His voice is barely above a whisper.

His eyes don't leave the photos. "She was playing in her room. Having a tea party before it was time for bed. I was about to get her into the bath. I knocked on her door to let her know I was getting the water going. She said okay and kept playing. Pretending to have tea with the Queen." He smiles a little at that. "When I went to get her, I opened the door to her room and she was gone."

His large hands clench into tight fists. And the fury coming off him is so heavy it's almost suffocating. "They left the bedroom window open."

He turns away from the pictures and walks away, heading for a hallway. I follow a bit behind him. He stops at an open door, and I come up behind him and peer around him. The space screams that it's a little girl's room. It's full of stuffed animals, and on the light-pink walls are paintings of mermaids and unicorns. The window is still open, the teal and silver curtains blowing in the breeze.

I look around, not really sure what to look for. I wasn't trained for this, but hopefully some of the *Law and Order* shows I've watched with my grandpa will help. I step into the room.

"I've combed this room for clues. I don't know what else you'll find," he tells me, sounding somewhat impatient. "I should be out there looking." He keeps looking at the window, almost like she'll just climb back through.

I scan the room, kinda hoping something just pops out at me. She's got some dolls laid out on the floor, along with coloring books, but that's it. Something's missing though. "She was having a tea party?" I ask, seeing only crayons scattered about. And why isn't the room more trashed? The crayons look like they were just put down next to the coloring book, not thrown about as if she fought someone. But where are the cups, the teapot?

"Yeah," he says, eyes still fixed on the curtains blowing in the breeze.

I move into his line of sight. "There's no tea set," I say.

"What?" he asks, moving into the room.

I point towards the floor. "There's no tea set. Does she have one?" I ask.

"Of course, we're English," he answers like I should know better, but he's staring at the floor as if the tea set will magically appear.

Why would she say she was having tea with the Queen if there's no tea? Did someone tell her to say that? But she's too little to be told what to say; she'd probably scream or start crying. He would have heard how scared she was...but he did hear her. He heard her voice.

My heart races and my head snaps to Robert. "When's the last time you actually *saw* her?" I ask, my suspicions piquing, my whole body vibrating.

He keeps staring at the floor, like he can see his daughter there playing with her tea set. "Right after dinner, when she went into her room to play," he says.

I step over to him and grab his arm. He's not getting how important my questions are. "Did she say she was going to do a tea party?" I ask with force.

He finally looks at me, his face completely confused. "No. I don't understand, what are you thinking?"

I want to shout at him about who could be behind it, but I have an overwhelming urge to call Mr. Smith. "I have an idea, but let me call Mr. Smith." I pull my phone out and dial his number. I should call him anyways, because I don't want to be wrong.

"Find something?" Mr. Smith asks as a way of answering the call.

"Maybe. I'm going to put you on speaker." I hit the speaker button. "You still there?" I ask.

"Yes. What are you thinking?" he asks.

I look at Robert, praying that I'm right and this is a lead. "I don't think that was your daughter in the room saying she was having a tea party." He starts to open his mouth to say something, but I cut him off. "I think it was Sariah."

"What makes you say that?" Mr. Smith asks slowly.

"There's no tea set on the ground. If she had been snatched while playing, it would still be there. Or at least scattered on the floor." Robert bends down, searching the floor, but he won't find anything.

"But how would she even be able to mimic her voice?" Mr. Smith asks.

Sariah has to hear the voice to know how to mimic it. A thought pops into my head. "Did you go anywhere today?" I ask Robert.

He runs an agitated hand through his hair. "Uh, we went to the corner shop to get biscuits and boiled sweets. We walked by the water for a bit."

"Sariah could have easily been following him today and he wouldn't have known. He hasn't even met her yet. Or she could listened at the window," I tell Mr. Smith.

"If it was Sariah imitating Poppy's voice, that means Poppy could be gone longer than we thought," Mr. Smith says carefully.

Robert covers his face with his hands and a sound of pure anguish rips out of him.

"I highly doubt Sariah flew in to England," Mr. Smith says. "Ever since we realized she walked out of Project Lightning, we've got her picture circulating at airports. She must be traveling a different way." I hear the clicking of a keyboard over the phone.

"Okay, this is what we're going to do; we'll switch to looking at video feeds from the docks in the area. There's a good chance they've already reached a boat," Mr. Smith says.

"Do you know how many water access points there are around here?" Robert asks, his voice heavy with frustration and a little defeat.

"Becca, give your phone to Robert. And take me off speaker."

I hand the phone over and look back into the room. There has to be something we've missed. I scan the floor, but it's still just the toys scattered about. I look at the dresser, covered in crayons, small figurines, and more drawings. *Come on, there must be something else.* I walk over to the unmade bed and a teddy bear lies on its side. I turn and look at the bedside table. There's a lamp, a book, and a power cord dangling over the side. I squat down and search the ground to see if maybe whatever was plugged in fell to the floor. Nothing. My heart starts to race. "Robert? What's connected to this?" I ask, holding the cord in my hand.

He looks at my hands, the phone still to his ear. "An older cell phone that I let her use to listen to music."

My whole body seems to shake with what this could mean. "Is it still connected to your account?" I hurriedly ask, wanting to jump up and shake this monster of a man.

"Yes." The hope in that one word rushes through me. Time seems to freeze as we both stare each other, but it's quickly broken as he drops my phone to the ground and starts digging his phone out of his pocket.

"Track it," I tell him unnecessarily. My whole body feels like a live wire. I want to grab the phone because I feel like I could do it faster than him.

I grab my cell off the ground and tell Mr. Smith what's happening.

"I've got her! She must have had it in her pocket!" he shouts, holding his phone up in the air.

I put the phone back on speaker. "Where's it showing her?" Mr. Smith asks, and I hear furious typing in the background.

"They're almost at Lock Lake. It's showing her on Fort Cumberland road. I'm heading over there," he says, and starts to head out of the bedroom.

I chase after him down the hall. "Wait. Show me. I can get there faster."

"That's too dangerous," I hear Mr. Smith bark from the phone.

I narrow my eyes at the phone, even though he can't see me. "And sending me to North Korea wasn't?" I yell back at him.

That seems to shut him up for a moment. "I need to do this, and you can track my phone. It's not like they can keep me contained," I say.

"Yes, but they could hurt Poppy," Robert tells me as he grabs his keys off the table and heads for the door.

"I won't let anything happen to her," I promise him, walking through the house with him.

He stops and looks into my eyes, and it feels a little like he's measuring my worth. He hands over his phone and I look at the map, trying to figure out where they might go next. I zoom out a little on the map and see a marina not too far from her location.

"I'm going to head toward Ferry road. There seem to be docks there," I say, pointing at the map. I hand the cell back to him.

"I won't be far behind you," he tells me, rushing out the door.

"Go, and be careful," I hear Mr. Smith say from the phone still clutched in my hand.

"I'll do my best. Track me and tell Robert where I am," I tell him, and then hang up.

I shake out my hands, desperately trying to get my nerves under control. I can't end up in the wrong place. I picture the map, where I want to go, and close my eyes.

ELEVEN

A brisk, cool breeze whooshes over my skin, and the musty smell of the lake and diesel fuel envelops me. I open my eyes, but it takes a minute to adjust to the darkness. I hear the brakes of a car and scrunch down next to a boat.

I slowly stand back up and look around. I'm in a parking lot, surrounded by a lot of boats, but they're all dry docked. I slowly walk to the front of the boat to see what's on the other side. Across the street it looks like there are a bunch more boats already bobbing in the water. They've got to be heading there with Poppy. I inch around the front of the boat, towards the road.

I can't really dart across the street, so...in a blink I'm standing next to a black sedan on the other side. I start walking towards where the boats are, and it seems there's only one way to get onto the dock. That's got to be their entrance point. I crouch down next to an old pickup truck and wait. Hopefully no security guard finds me.

A minute later a white van drives by, slowing at the parking lot for the dock. Seriously, is that what they're driving? Man, bad guys need to get more original with their car choices.

Three car doors slam and I shimmy my way around the truck to get a better look. Sariah stands there with two men. One of the guys hefts a huge duffle bag up over his shoulder. That's got to be Poppy. Sariah waves her hands around, but I can't really hear her. All I hear is the water lapping softly at my back. I transport a little closer so I can make out what she's saying.

My heart is thudding so loudly in my chest as I transport behind a little red car. My nerves are twisting and firing so violently, I'll be lucky to not get sick all over the pavement.

"I didn't agree to this," Sariah whisper-shouts to one of the men. I move a little closer, trying my best to step lightly.

"Well, sweetheart"—whoa, judging by his tone, he does not think very highly of her— "what did you think was going to happen when you double-crossed them?" the one not holding Poppy asks. His voice is thick with impatience.

"No one said anything about kids," she tells him, her voice harsh and accusing. She doesn't fear this guy; she just sounds mad.

"You said *whatever it takes*." He gestures towards the duffle bag. "This is what it's going to take. There's no going back now anyways." He leans closer to her face with those words.

Sariah makes a grunt of frustration, but she doesn't say anything else. I can't believe she'd let someone take a little girl. Why is she even working with these guys?

They start to move away from the van. I wring my hands together. If they get on the boat with Poppy, we might never find her again. What am I going to do? Especially when there are three of them. I look around, hoping to see Robert magically appear, but there's no sign of him. He said he wouldn't be far.

With each step they take towards the dock, my stomach knots tighter. I've got to do something. I transport right behind the car closest to the entrance. Maybe I can transport onto the boat? Then what? I can't transport with her. I drag my hands down my face. This is a mess.

A soft splash to my left makes me almost jump into air. "Becca," a man whispers, and it takes all of my self-control not to scream.

I kneel down to get a better look into the water and Robert's head is there, staring back at me with water dripping down his face. It's too dark to see under the water, but he definitely doesn't have a scuba mask or anything. "What—" I start to ask, but he cuts me off.

"Later," he tells me. "We need a plan, and fast."

"Got it." Not really, but I'll do what he tells me.

"I'm going to swim to where they're headed. I need you to transport in front of them and distract them." I look at the dock they just entered.

"Then what?" I ask, because what if one of them pulls out a gun and shoots me or something?

"We're just going to have to wing it," he says.

Awesome. Great plan.

I know he's not thinking things through. I have no clue how I'd act if I had a kid that was kidnapped. Probably crazy.

"Our focus is Poppy. Once I've got her, you get the hell out of there," he orders me. His authoritative voice immediately gets me nodding my head. And technically we didn't get a direct order to grab one of them. Plus I don't have a clue how I'd do that.

"Give me a few minutes' head start and then go distract them. As soon as I've got her, I'll meet you three miles down the beach that way," he points in direction I need to head. "Start counting," he says, and then slips back into the water.

I watch for him to surface again, but he doesn't. He's got to be like Aquaman or something.

I count to sixty twice, keeping my eyes on the group making their way past the guard shack, while the butterflies in my stomach turn to bats and threaten to eat me from the inside out. They're getting too far. I've gotta go now. In a blink of an eye I'm popping right in front of them.

"Hi," I say, and give a little wave.

The three of them freeze, but it doesn't last. Sariah is the first to react. The other two stay back. She takes a step forward, but stops and scans the area around us. I'm virtually alone, but she doesn't need to know that. "They sent *you*?" she asks, like the idea of me being here is the stupidest thing she's ever heard.

"I'm the fastest."

"Come to play hero, then?" she taunts.

"Something like that." I quickly scan the water for Robert, but there's nothing.

"What are you looking at?" she asks, looking towards the water.

I step forward, closer into her space, trying to get her attention back on me. Her eyes snap to me with the movement. "Where's Tony?" I ask, my voice low, angry.

Her face breaks out in the cockiest smirk. "We need her alive, Ben," she says, ignoring my question. "But they never said she had to be unharmed." Her face suddenly turns to stone. I'm not getting any information out of her. Not like I thought I would, but it was worth a try.

"You can't contain me." I know I sound arrogant, but it's true.

"No, but we can make you comply," Ben says. "Derek, throw our package into the water."

Derek lifts the duffle off his shoulder. "No!" I scream, wanting to lunge for it, but Sariah and Ben stand in the way.

Ben makes a *tsking* noise at me. "No? Well, you better get on our boat. And if you transport away at any time, I can't guarantee she'll make it to our destination," Ben says, his mouth twisted into a cruel smile. Does he get a kick out of all of this?

"Killing kids now?" I ask Sariah, my eyes never leaving that duffle.

She ignores my question and looks back to the water. She can't find Robert; it'll ruin everything.

"Bet your mom would be *real* proud," I say, and that does the trick.

She whips back around and goes to throw a punch, but I quickly step back. "You do not get to talk about my mother!" Sariah screams at me.

I glance at the duffle that Derek is holding over the water. This would be the perfect time for Robert to intervene.

"As entertaining as this all is...tick-tock, darling." Ben drawls.

Anytime now, Robert. Any. Time.

I jump in place for a second, trying to buy time...I've got no clue what I'm doing, but I know I can't let either of us get on that boat.

"Why is she acting weird?" Sariah asks the two guys, and then looks at me. "Why are you acting weird?"

"Uh." I hold my hands up in a confused gesture.

The sound of splashing water makes all of us look over to right. Robert leaps out of the water with a battle cry holding a bowie knife, and in a move that I swear defies the law of physics, stabs Derek in the side that holds Poppy. He immediately drops the bag to clutch at the wound, and Robert snatches the bag midair, and lands on his back in water. He propels himself backward, keeping the duffle above water. But he's quickly out of eyesight.

"You little—" Ben begins to say as he advances on me. And I'd like to say that I'm about to use all the moves that Gregory taught me, but all I can think of is to kick him in the junk. So I do, and super hard too.

He drops to his knees, groaning in agony. Sariah and I look at each other. "See you soon," I vow to her. And I get the hell out of there.

TWELVE

I transport to what I'm hoping is three miles down the beach like Robert said. I stand on the sand and look around. It's hard to see anything in this darkness.

A splash to my left startles me and I look towards it. I can just make out the outline of Robert wading in the water, and he's carrying Poppy. I rush over to them.

"Is she okay?" I ask as I come to a stop next to him.

He moves farther up on the shore, and I follow along next to him. She looks like she's sleeping. "They gave her something to knock her out, probably chloroform. I'll know for sure when Xavier gets to my house."

"You're going back there?" I ask, because this doesn't seem like the greatest idea.

"We both are," he tells me as he heads towards the road.

"We are?" Why does he need me to stay?

"I'm going to need your help, and as soon as the rest of the team gets here we'll head back to my home. They won't attack again if there are more of us. For now we're going to stay at a budget hotel not far from here." He turns and walks parallel to the road, and I just follow along, wondering why he needs my help with and not really sure he's firing on all cylinders.

"But what if they're waiting for you at the house and follow you? And why do you need my help at the hotel?" Why does he seem so calm about this?

"There's an escape tunnel from the house that leads to the naval base, and I need to grab some things from home before we leave." Well, that's convenient. "We'll have to figure out a diversion when Gregory and the rest get here, but it should be enough time to get us to the base and then escape. I need you at the hotel as a cover."

He stops next to a car. "Under the wing are the car keys. Grab them, will you? I'm going to have you drive while I sit in the back with her."

"Wing?" There's a wing on a car? What the heck is the wing?

"The fender. The keys are on top of the wheel on the driver's side door."

I walk to the driver's door, but Robert's words halt me in my tracks. "Wrong side," he tells me.

I hurry to the other side, muttering under my breath about how most of the world drives on the right side of the road.

"Where are you going to go after?" I ask after I unlock the doors.

He carefully lays Poppy down on the back seat and I watch as his hand smooths down her hair. A pang goes through my chest. I wonder if my dad would have risked himself to save me. And I wonder, if he'd had the chance, would he smooth my hair with the gentlest hand like Robert's doing with Poppy?

"I've been trying to figure that out," he says, bringing me out my thoughts.

"You could go to headquarters," I offer.

He pauses, but then shakes his head. "That's probably not a good idea," he says, still looking at Poppy.

"Why not?" I ask.

He stands up and runs his hands over the top of his head, sending water in all directions. "My house isn't even under my name, but they still found us here. Everyone would know if I showed up there."

He doesn't know about the stolen data? Mr. Smith didn't tell the ones with kids? Does he know about the missing children? Should I tell him? I kind of want to, but what if that causes an avalanche of problems? Even if they knew beforehand, the name being different on the house doesn't matter; they would have found him anyways. "Are you going to tell Mr. Smith where you're going?"

"Of course," he says without hesitation. "I trust he'll keep the information to himself." He studies my face. "Why do you look so unsure?"

I didn't even know I looked that way, but I'm not surprised he can see it. "I guess I don't know him that well. He comes off like..." Is it okay to essentially insult your boss to a guy you barely know? I mean, saving someone's kid is kind of a bonding experience, so maybe it's okay?

"A prat?" he asks.

"Uh, sure, whatever that means."

He laughs and I swear I hear him mutter, "American." But he quickly sobers. "I trust him with Poppy's life," he tells me, his voice heavy with the truth of that statement.

We stare at one another, him showing me how much he trusts Mr. Smith, and me nodding that I get it.

"Hop in the driver's seat. I've got some dry clothes in the boot to change into real quick," he tells me, breaking the tension.

I get in the car and keep my eyes focused on the road ahead. I hear the trunk open and close. This is super awkward. I look into the rearview mirror at the sound of the door closing. "All right, let's get out of here," he tells me.

"Okay, where am I going?" I ask as I start up the car.

"Before we go anywhere, don't forget which side of the road to drive on. Once you've got that, drive up the road a bit and take a left," he tells me.

I follow the rest of his directions and fifteen minutes later we pull into a parking lot of a six-story hotel.

"We're staying here? What's our story we're telling the clerk? How are you going to explain an unconscious child?" I ask, rapidly firing the questions at him without giving him a chance to answer.

"Rebecca, relax," he tells me, and I notice my hands are strangling the steering wheel.

I take a deep breath and try to relax my tense body. I'm still so on edge from what happened at the dock that I'm acting all crazy.

"Just act like I'm your brother and everything will be fine. I'll check us in and handle it. Just go along with it," he tells me, sounding self-assured. I'm glad one of us is.

"Okay. Sure." *Go along with it?* Let's see how good my acting skills are.

We get out the car and Robert walks to the trunk, Poppy cradled in his arms against his chest. "Open the boot and pull out the bag back there."

"Why?"

"Because it'll look a tad wonky if we're getting a room without some luggage."

"Good point," I say, and grab the bag from the trunk.

We lock up the car and head towards the lobby. *Everything is going to be fine. Just act natural.*

As soon as we walk in through the automatic doors, my mental chant crumbles. I'm going to blow this for us. What if I flicker? How can I act like his sister when I'm American? *For crying out loud, get it together.*

"Hey. It'll be fine. We're not doing anything wrong," he tells me in a soft voice. I bet this is how he talks to Poppy when she's scared.

I shoot him a grateful smile and pull my crap together.

We approach the reception desk and are greeted by a middle-aged guy whose tag says his name is Ian and apparently he's also the manager. He's dressed in a suit and has a super bright smile on his face.

"Welcome to South Sea Hotel. Checking in, I presume," Ian says.

"Yes, but we don't have reservations. We just got into town and a need a room for the night," Robert says.

He bounces Poppy in his arms and makes a shushing noise like she's starting to wake up. "Shh, sweet girl," he says to her.

Whoa. He's way too good at this. And now that I think about it, he's kinda too good-looking to be a dad. I shake the thought away.

"One room?" Ian asks, eyeing me.

"Yes, a double though. This one"—his head dips towards Poppy —"can sleep with her auntie." I have the ridiculous urge to wave or do something else awkward, but I check myself and just keep a smile on my face. I'm not good at this stuff. Apparently I can infiltrate a military compound in enemy territory, but I suck at acting.

"All right, if you'll just give me your card, we'll bill you once you check out tomorrow."

Robert looks at me expectantly.

"Uh, I don't have my wallet on me," I try to tell him in my best attempt at an English accent. And either the manager is too nice to say anything or I pulled it off.

I'm failing miserably, because Robert starts coughing into his shoulder like he's trying to disguise a laugh.

He clears his throat a few times before he finally seems to have himself under control. "Bet you left it at mum's house again. That's fine, just grab mine out of my back pocket."

I reach into his back pocket—which is super awkward, by the way —as fast as I can. I hand over the card to the manager.

"You are all set for room twenty-five on the first floor," he says after running it.

"Thank you," Robert says, and I grab the card back and hold on to it. I don't really feel like reaching into his pocket again.

We turn towards the hall and I head for the rooms, but Robert stops at the elevator.

"Didn't he say the first floor?" I ask, trying to keep my voice low so no one overhears me.

"Yes, but this is the ground floor. We need to go up one," he tells me.

"Weird British people," I mutter under my breath.

"Maybe you Americans have it all wrong," he tells me as we step onto the elevator.

"Yeah, yeah."

"Your accent, though..." He trails off, laughing.

"Guess I missed Undercover Spy 101 at headquarters."

We make our way off the elevator and down the hall to our room. Freezing cold air and the ever-present hotel-room smell greets us when we open the door. I flip a light on and see an ordinary room with two beds.

Robert carefully lowers Poppy to one of the beds. He takes his time brushing the hair off her face and making sure she's tucked underneath the covers.

"Do you think she'll be out for much longer?" I ask. I hope she's okay. She's so little. And all I can think about are those pictures over the fireplace where she's laughing, beaming at the camera with her bright smile.

He wraps his large hand around her small wrist. "Her pulse is good. She should wake up soon," he tells me, and his voice is so sure that it makes me believe him.

I sit on the opposite bed and pull my phone out of my pocket. "Crap, we need to call Mr. Smith," I say. I've got multiple missed calls and a few texts telling me to call immediately.

"Call and put him on speaker," he tells me.

I tap on his name and the line doesn't even have a chance to ring before Mr. Smith's voice booms through the speaker. "Why the hell haven't you been answering your phone?" If a phone could shake from the anger in a voice, my phone would be across the room. Mr. Smith is beyond pissed.

"Sorry. Kind of busy rescuing Poppy and fleeing the area," I tell him—a little flippant, but he *was* tracking me.

I can clearly hear the deep breath he takes. I bet he's sitting at his cluttered desk, rubbing his temples.

"So you have her?" he asks.

I look at Poppy lying on the bed like she just fell asleep. Do kids always look smaller and more fragile while they're sleeping? "Yes, I'm here with Poppy and Robert," I tell him.

"Sir," Robert says, stepping away from the bed with his daughter and closer to me.

"Debrief, and tell me why you're at a hotel," Mr. Smith orders.

"We intercepted them at the docks," Robert begins, then continues to recount the events while I stand there. He doesn't embellish, just gets straight to the facts.

"Was anyone apprehended?" Mr. Smith asks. My eyes shoot to Robert's.

"No" is Robert's only answer.

"Was there an opportunity?" Mr. Smith asks, and I guess if someone else had been there besides us there technically would have been, but I wasn't grabbing anyone and Robert had his hands full.

Robert takes a deep breath and his whole body tightens like he's preparing himself for Mr. Smith's response to whatever he's about to say. "My priority was Poppy."

"Is she well?" Mr. Smith asks, and Robert's shoulders drop at his question. I bet he thought he was going to get an earful.

"They knocked her out, but she should be coming around soon," Robert says, his voice steady.

"Any luck for you, Becca?" Mr. Smith asks.

"Well, they were holding Poppy out over the water like they were going to let her drown, so I'm not really sure what you wanted me to do. Plus three against one are awful odds."

"And was it Sariah?" Mr. Smith asks, ignoring my sarcasm.

"Yeah. And two other guys I haven't seen before. Ben and Derek."

"Luckily, Xavier will be there soon. We'll be able to know if they're the same guys that took Tony," Mr. Smith says.

I wish Gregory had been there. He would have been able to read Sariah's mind. We could have found Tony. There's so much we could have learned.

"The rest of the team should arrive in the next five hours," Mr. Smith tells us.

"When they get here, I want them escorting us to my home," Robert says, brooking no argument.

"You going to head to base from there?" Mr. Smith asks.

"Yes," Robert answers.

"Good. Contact me when you get there," Mr. Smith tells him.

"Yes, sir."

"I'll talk to you after the others get there." The call ends before either of us can say anything else.

Robert drops down on the end of Poppy's bed. His whole body seems to collapse in on itself. "You should get some sleep," he tells me.

I don't know how he thinks I'll be able to sleep after all of that. "I'll stay up until Poppy comes around," I say.

He waves off my offer. "Trust me; you're going to need it. If I know Mr. Smith, he'll have you going somewhere else soon. And with your ability, you can guarantee it. You need to get rest whenever and wherever you can. Sadly, it won't be long until you'll be able to make yourself fall asleep anywhere."

I lie down, but I can't sleep, so I watch a father care for his daughter. He pulls the blanket up higher on her and then brushes her hair back from her face. He leans farther over and gently kisses her temple. Is this how it would have been with my dad? Would he have gone to these lengths for me? It's such a crushing blow to realize that I'll never get to know either way, but for tonight, I'll pretend.

THIRTEEN

A soft touch to my shoulder is what drags me out of sleep. "They're on their way up," a voice says softly.

I turn towards it and open my eyes. Robert's kind face looks back at me. I look past him and see Poppy. She's lying on her side, staring at me with wide eyes. I give her a little wave, and she burrows herself deeper into her blankets. I sit up and rub at my eyes. My body protests a little. Even though I've been asleep for several hours, I didn't get enough sleep.

Robert follows my stare towards his daughter. "This is Rebecca," he tells her.

She studies me from her blanket cocoon.

"She helped find you. She's a friend," he tells her. His voice is soothing, loving.

I reach out and put a hand on his arm. "It's okay," I tell him. If I were her I probably wouldn't want anyone near me right now. She must be so scared, even though her dad is here.

A knock at the door has all of us turning our heads, but the small cry makes us look back. Robert rushes over to his daughter and starts saying soothing words I can't hear. I slide off the bed and head for the door.

I look through the peephole and Gregory waves at me from the other side.

Poppy's really scared right now.

He gives me a thumbs up, and I can hear his voice murmur to the others.

I pull open the door and look at their disheveled appearances. I know for sure I don't look any better. As it is, I don't know how much more my body can take all this hopping around. I'm also probably in desperate need of a shower.

They walk into the room, and as Gregory passes by me, his hand quickly grazes mine. That little bolt of lightning hits me, and I'm just going to pretend it was because he's one of the hundred, and not anything more.

Robert stands from the bed and Raven reaches him first, giving him a huge hug. "I'm so sorry," she says softly.

"We got her back," he tells her in a fierce voice.

Xavier and Gregory step forward and do the handshake-slap-on-the-back "man" thing. "I'm so glad you guys got here quickly," Robert says.

"I wish we could have been here sooner," Gregory tells him, eyes looking at Poppy.

Xavier walks closer to Poppy and squats down next to the bed. "Hey, little bug," he says, his rough voice gentle.

"Uncle X," she whispers to him.

"It won't happen again," he vows.

"Becca," Gregory says, and I shift my eyes to him. "Come out in the hall with me?" he asks.

I follow him out the door, and as soon as it closes he pulls me into his arms. I take a deep breath and let my body collapse into his for a moment. "Does it ever stop?" I ask into his shoulder.

He rubs his hand up and down my back. "What?" he asks.

"The constant insanity. The fear. I feel like I'm on the edge of a panic attack or breakdown all the time. I never used to be like this. I could handle whatever was thrown at me, but now...now I feel like I'm back in freshman year of high school and I walked into class without any clothes on."

"What we do is the epitome of high stress, but right now it's even more than it's ever been," he says.

Of course it is.

I pull away from his arms, needing the separation but at the same time missing it. "Mr. Smith filled you in on the plan?" I ask.

"Yeah. We're going to leave here soon. I want to get a read on Poppy, and Xavier wants to check out her room too, and the dock."

"Do you really need to read her?" I ask. Because that little girl has already been through so much.

"It'll be a lot easier for her to show me what happened than having to tell anyone," he says.

"If you say so." I'm not even sure how much he can do with mind reading, but I wonder if he can *see* what people see in their thoughts or just hear them.

We make our way back into the room and Gregory walks over to Poppy's side. Robert talks with Raven in the corner, while Xavier sits next to Poppy on the bed, his phone out in front of them. They laugh at whatever's on the screen.

"Hey, bug," Gregory says as he crouches down next to her.

Does everyone have such a close connection?

She gives Gregory a tentative smile. "Show me?" he asks. And this must not be the first time they've done this, because she nods her head and closes her eyes.

The room quiets as we watch the pair. Gregory's face morphs from anger to sadness and back again. But as Poppy starts to open her eyes, he puts a small smile on his face. "You did great. Thanks for showing me, bug."

He ruffles the hair on the top of her head and then rises up from her side of the bed. He crosses over to Robert. "Ready to head to the house?" Gregory asks.

"Yeah. I want to grab some things. No clue when we'll be back," he says.

"We've got a car out front," Gregory says. "I'll take Becca; Raven and Xavier will go in yours. Once we pull up, get in the house quick. Does that work?"

"It's a plan," Robert says. He walks over to Poppy. "Up you go," he tells her as he scoops her up in his arms.

"Do we need to check out?" I ask.

"Mr. Smith will take care of it," Gregory assures me.

We all file out of the room and walk towards the stairs at the end of the all. It leads us straight out into the back parking lot. We walk the group to Robert's car, and once they're safely inside, Gregory and I head over to a black town car.

I slide into the passenger seat, making sure it's the correct side, and wait for Gregory to acknowledge the fifty million questions flying around in my head.

"It pretty much happened like you thought it did," he tells me. "Except Sariah made herself sound like Robert at the window. That's why Poppy went and opened it. She thought maybe he was playing a game or a joke."

I would have done the same thing, even now. Man, that's a scary thought. "How awful," I say.

He nods his head, but his eyes stay on the road as we head back to Robert's.

"You guys all know Poppy?" I ask.

"Since she was born."

Why weren't any of them around when I was growing up? I could have had a heads up about the life I was going to fall into.

"Poppy's mom died giving birth to her, and Rob took it pretty bad. He was in a really dark place. Can't really blame him. But he doesn't have any family like you do, so we all stepped in to help him out."

"It still irks me that you do that," I tell him. I don't know if I'll ever get used to my thoughts not being private. I look out the window, but I highly doubt I'm going to see a creepy white van following us.

"Not all the time," he points out. His eyes constantly flick to the mirror, watching Robert's car behind us. But he's got a point.

"You're right. Sometimes it's convenient." And it has been, and it probably will be again in the future. I know that. I just haven't really accepted it.

"I can't turn it on and off." He tries to stress the importance of those words. And I get it, but it doesn't make it any easier. It's just another thing we have to figure out. All relationships have to make some adjustments; why not have powers to contend with?

"What's the plan?" I ask, trying to turn the conversation back to the problem at hand because I think we're almost to the house.

"We'll get them inside and through the tunnel, and then we'll stay in his house for a bit until we can figure out whether or not they're watching the place."

"So sit and wait?" I ask.

"Sit and wait," he confirms.

We pull up in front of Robert's home, and once we step out of the car, the rest follow. Xavier stalks to the front door. "I'm going to make a sweep," he says, eyes focused on the house, moving like he'll tackle anything that crosses his path.

"Don't bother, no one is here," Gregory calls after him.

"You never know," is Xavier's cool response.

"It'll make him feel better," I whisper to Gregory.

He looks over at me and nods. I'm sure he knows that too.

Xavier disappears into the house and the rest of us follow behind him. "Let's go pick out some of your things," Robert tells Poppy, while the rest of us stand in the living room.

Raven watches them walk away and her face looks so sad. I'm surprised how much she shows her emotions. I figured years of being with Project Lightning would jade people, but apparently not her.

Robert and Poppy only take a few minutes and then they're back in the living room, each with a backpack. Robert squats down and looks into Poppy's eyes. "We'll be back," he tells her.

Xavier walks back into the room. "Everything looks fine. I don't think anyone's been back here. Ready to go?" he asks them.

Robert nods and they walk to another door in the hallway. "Mr. Smith will let you guys know when we're in the clear. Stay safe." He takes a moment to look the three of them in the eye. And then his gaze lands on me. "I owe you, Becca." He looks down at Poppy. "More than you'll ever know." He keeps looking at Poppy as they walk through the door in the hall.

Where are they—

"Basement," Gregory tells me before I can even finish my thought.

"Settle in," Xavier says, and he makes himself at home on the couch.

"What happens next?" I ask.

"Xavier needs to check out the dock, and then we're heading back to the States. To Sariah's house," Gregory tells me.

His phone dings in his pocket. He looks at it and his eyes shift over to me.

"He wants me to transport back." I don't even bother phrasing it as a question, because I know the answer.

"Yeah," Gregory says.

I drag a hand over my face. "This is killing my body's time clock. I don't even know what day it is."

I stand from the couch and stretch my arms over my head. "Will you shoot him a text and tell him I'm on my way?" I ask Gregory, and when I turn towards him I see his eyes fixed on the sliver of skin showing above my jeans.

Eyes up here.

He gives his head a little shake and looks away from my stomach. "Uh, yeah. Sorry." He starts typing away on his phone.

I shake my head at him, laughing softly. "See you guys soon," I tell them.

I close my eyes and picture the door to Mr. Smith's office. The pull on my body only lasts an instant, and in the blink of an eye I find myself in front of a familiar door.

FOURTEEN

"Busy day," Mr. Smith says without looking up from the computer on his desk as I walk into the office.

I drop down heavily in the chair in front of his desk. "Every day seems like a busy day."

He finally looks up at me. His face looks drawn and tired. Aren't we a matching pair? "It's not always this way. Lately it just seems..." He rocks back in his office chair, trying to find a description of the insanity lately.

"Ridiculous? Exhausting? Deadly?" I offer.

"Ramped up," he says in deadpan voice.

That's an understatement. But at least I'm functioning and not cowering in my room. If I can just keep my focus on finding Tony and helping kids like Bronia and Poppy, I think I'll be okay. Maybe. Hopefully.

"So am I waiting for the team to get back here or are you sending me somewhere else?" I ask, and I'm hoping he says to go back to my room, because I'm exhausted.

"They're going to be leaving soon for North Carolina, for Sariah's house. You'll meet them there. But for now, relax, eat, go sleep, give yourself a chance to wind down. You've got twelve hours before they're in North Carolina, and then I need you back here."

I swear my whole body gives at the word sleep. I was being serious when I told Gregory I had no clue what day it was. This can't be good for my body. And all this transporting feels like it's draining my energy. Maybe I'm just not used to it.

I give him a mock salute and transport to my room. I kick off my shoes and crash onto my bed, fully clothed. I could care less that I smell like a mixture of the ocean and day-old sweaty clothing; sleep is pulling me under fast, and I'm okay with that.

"CAN'T I just have a normal dream that's a smash-up of everything going on in my mind right now like everyone else?"

"I'm not really sure I control this," Mom tells me.

We're sitting on a dock, much like the one I was on last night. But we're at a lake instead of out by the ocean. The air smells heavily of wet earth and pond scum.

"What's with all the water locations lately?" I ask her, my feet dangling over the edge as I stare at the dark depths below that.

"Maybe because water is soothing?" She doesn't seem to have any better answer.

Unbidden, I see a duffle sinking. I shake my head, Poppy's fine. Robert got to her in time.

"Did you know Sariah's mom?" I ask, my eyes staying on the water, watching for anything else to pop up.

"Of course," she says. I see the reflection of her feet dangling next to mine.

I motion with my hand for her to tell me more.

"What do you want to know?" she asks, her voice hesitant.

"Sariah seems like such an angry person. Is that what her mom was like? Do you know what mission her mom was on when she died?"

"I haven't seen her in several years. The only one I kept any kind

of contact with was Ania, so I wouldn't know about her last mission, but she wasn't an angry person. She was so excited when she found out she was pregnant with Sariah. But are you really surprised at how mad Sariah is?" she asks.

"She's not the only one who lost a parent though," I say, leaving out the fact that I lost both.

"People deal with grief differently," she tells me. I can feel her eyes on me, but I won't look at her. We both know how she dealt with the death of my dad. And I'm not sure I can ever really forgive her for that.

She lets out a sad sigh.

"Got any more cryptic wisdom?" I ask.

"Be open-minded," she tells me, and I can't help but laugh at that.

I finally look over at her. "I feel like all I get from you is bad fortune-cookie advice."

"How about one last fortune?" she asks hurriedly while she looks around.

I follow her gaze and see thunderheads rolling in. She reaches out and grips my arm. It jars me because it feels so real. "Don't be afraid of meeting new people. Give it a chance." Her words are vague, and yet her stare is piercing. She's trying to tell me something important. She's warning me.

A strong wind pushes at our backs. The clouds have moved eerily close to us. She stands up quickly. "Until next time," she says, her gaze lingering on me. She takes off down the dock at a fast clip and a bolt of lightning hits the water. Whoa, that's close. I shut my eyes; it's time to wake up...now.

I HEAD BACK towards Mr. Smith's office. I can't believe I slept for ten hours. The dream with my mom is still lingering like a bad taste in my mouth. She seemed hesitant to tell me that last bit of information. Is someone coming? But how would she know that? There's no way.

The sight of Mr. Smith's door stops all thoughts of my mom. I knock and immediately hear him tell me to enter.

He's at his desk again, and I have to wonder: does the man ever sleep? Does he have a home? And why does this feel like *Groundhog Day*? Every time I wake up I'm walking into this office.

"Did you get some rest?" is his version of a greeting.

"I slept" is the answer I give him. Because I don't know if I'm actually getting rest when I have these dreams with Mom. If anything, I sometimes feel even more drained when I have them.

"Did Xavier find anything in England?" I ask. He's had to have had enough time to talk to him.

He draws in a deep breath and releases it slowly. "Whoever Sariah is working with is making sure they're meticulous in what they're doing. Nothing pertinent was mentioned at either location. We've either got to hope someone messes up or that Sariah's dad will have something for us."

I pinch the bridge of my nose and squeeze my eyes tight. We need to catch a break. "I hope so. I promised her I'd see her again soon," I tell him.

He flashes me a quick, ugly smirk before his face becomes serious again. "Good. Are you ready to go to Sariah's house and search her room?" he asks.

"After what happened with Poppy—yes."

"You won't meet up with them for a couple more hours. Get some food in you, get in a workout. Gregory will text you when it's time.

"Here's a blank jump drive. See if you can copy the hard drive if she's got a computer, but it's okay if you can't." He hands the drive to me over the desk and I put it in my pocket.

"Got it," I say.

"Now get out of here," he says, his focus going back to a screen on his desk.

I walk out of his office and head straight to my room, but I'm not planning on staying. That dream with my mom has Ania on my mind, and I need to go see if Walter heeded my warnings.

I drop my cell on my nightstand and close my eyes, keeping the image of Walter's backyard in my mind. In a blink I can feel sun beating on my back. I turn towards the house.

It looks like Walter fixed the back door Bronia ripped off. Brand new hinges shine against the chipped white paint. I walk up the back steps and look through the door's window into the kitchen that hasn't been updated since the seventies. Fake wood countertops and flat white cabinets fill the space, along with a lovely (not really) floral linoleum floor. There are a couple dirty dishes in the sink, a box of cereal on the counter, and a crossword sitting on the table. Why haven't they left?

I knock on the door and wait. No one comes to answer it. The house is too quiet. I should at least hear them moving around. But there are no footsteps or calls that they're coming.

I walk to the side of the house and look into the driveway. There's a small red truck sitting under a carport, but where are they? I head to the back door again and check the knob. It turns in my hand without hesitation.

"Walter? Bronia?" I call their names as I open the door a little.

Complete silence greets me.

I move into the kitchen and nothing looks out of place. There's still a faint lingering smell of bacon in the air. This whole thing feels off. "Hello? It's Becca," I call into the house. Last thing I want is a freaked-out ten-year-old with crazy strength jumping me.

The living room is ahead and I walk into it. Worn leather coaches flank a smaller television, with a wood coffee table between them. It's covered with a jigsaw puzzle that looks to be in the middle of being done. I touch the coffee table and a fine layer of dusts sits on top. It's odd, considering how tidy the house is.

I swear it's like aliens came and just abducted them. They aren't here; that's obvious now. But where did they go? And how long ago?

I stare at the jigsaw puzzle, not really seeing it, but trying to figure all this out. But something about that puzzle makes me look closer. It looks like someone was organizing it a little, but there are pieces scattered all around. I walk around the coffee table, trying to figure out why it looks odd. Maybe if—that's it. I rush to the kitchen, grab a chair, and drag it back. I stand on it and look down on the puzzle. As I squint my eyes, I see it. A large portion of the pieces are arranged in an arrow, and it's pointing towards the bookshelf.

I scramble off the chair and rush over to the books. Now what? I scan the books, looking for a clue, a flashing sign, anything. But I'm not seeing anything. Maybe my mind made the arrow appear? No. I shake my head. That was a definite arrow. I just have to focus.

I start tipping each book out, looking for anything. Finally on the third shelf, a slip of paper falls out when I tug on the book *Paradise Lost*. I read the words aloud: "Call me."

That's it? I turn the paper over, but there's nothing else. He told me the number to call, but what was it? I pace around the living room. "Was it 506? No, it didn't start that way. It was like 203," I mutter to myself.

I destroyed that paper like he said. I grab his house phone and hit the redial button. Maybe he left another clue. The line rings a few times until someone picks it up. "Stella's Pizza, can you hold?" a girl says over the line, and I hang up. That was a bust.

The sound of a car's brakes makes my head snap to the front window. I squat down and look through the slats in the blinds. A black minivan sits in front of the house. I've got to go. I need to get back before Mr. Smith looks for me to send me to Sariah's. I put the phone back on its holder and grab the note from Walter. Right before I transport I mess up the puzzle on the coffee table, just in case. Footsteps sound near the door, but I'm gone before anyone even knows I was there.

FIFTEEN

My heart's still pounding when I get back to headquarters. It was probably nothing. It's not like bad guys usually drive minivans, right? I mean, if I was up to something I'd drive something else. Or maybe I'd want to blend in, so a minivan would be a great cover. Man, if I keep going down this conspiracy theorist road, I'm going to drive myself insane.

I shake out my arms. I can't really tell anyone what happened. I wasn't even supposed to be there. So I'm going to take Mr. Smith's advice and go grab some food, and we'll blame my shakiness on needing sugar. I head for the cafeteria, hoping since it's an odd time, no one will be there.

I walk inside and see that Dex is here, loading up a plate at the salad bar. I guess if I'm going to run into anyone, I don't mind it being him. After the last time with Mike almost crying and everyone staring at me, I've been avoiding everyone. "Hey, Dex," I call out, my voice a little higher than it should be. Hopefully he won't notice.

He turns around, a smile on his face, and waves at me. I grab a plate and join him at the buffet. "How's it going, Becca?" he asks.

"Going fine," I tell him, and I hope I've got a great poker face.

Because things aren't fine. At least I'm not diving under a table, but I'm so on edge that I'm afraid I'll get an ulcer. I want to tell him what's going on. I want to warn him, but for now I'll load my plate and sit down to eat with Dex.

"I feel like I'm always running into you when I think no one else is going to be around," I say, and he chuckles.

We walk to the closest table and sit across from one another, digging into our food. "I was so busy at the lab that when I looked up I saw that I missed lunch."

"Does that happen a lot?" I ask after I swallow the bite in my mouth.

His cheeks redden and he adjusts the glasses on his face. "I can't help it. I just get in this zone where I have to figure out everything a mineral can do, and what *I* can do to it so it's more."

I'm jealous. He's doing things that are going to change the world. And at times I feel like, what am I bringing to the table?

He abruptly stops mid-bite. "Oh, I've been looking up that thing we talked about. Apparently there's a stone called carnelian. Supposedly it can block mind reading. If we can get our hands on some, I can see if it'll work." His voice is super animated, and he's waving his hands around, and I'm watching his fork, which is loaded with food.

"That's awesome. Where can we get it?" I ask, and I breathe a sigh of relief when he puts the fork in his mouth.

"Actually it's from Brazil, but I'm pretty sure I can just order it online. Though, I've come to find that it's better if it's straight from the source, but let's start with the stuff I can find."

"Can't we just visit the Amazon online rather than in person? I know nothing about mining and the Amazon seems like a scary place," I say. Brazil? Fantastic, because I really want to go digging around the Amazon Rainforest.

He snorts out a laugh. "Good one," he starts to laugh to himself, saying, "Amazon online" under his breath.

But if he could find the exact location in Brazil... "Hey Dex, do you think you can try and find the exact location of a mine? Or wherever we can find it?"

"Definitely."

We fall into a companionable silence, both focusing our food for the next ten minutes.

I stand up and pick up my tray. "Good. Next time I'm back, I'll come find you," I tell him.

"Leaving again?" he asks.

"Always going somewhere," I tell him.

"See you soon," he says, and goes back to his salad.

I dump my tray and head out the double doors. With no one around, I transport back to my room. I've still got some time before Gregory calls.

I sit on my bed and try to rack my brain for the number Walter gave me. I'm sure they're okay, but he left me that note.

My phone buzzes. It's a text from Gregory.

Almost to the meeting point. Transport on over.

I send him back a thumbs-up and bring up the pictures of the creepy school on my cell phone. Just looking at this place gives me the chills. I look past some of the buildings that are in use and the ones left to rot, and focus on the copse of trees we picked to meet at near the road leading to campus. At least the trees should help hide me. It's a pretty good rendezvous spot. I feel the pull of my body, and quickly cool wind washes across my skin and the overwhelming scent of pine envelopes me. Birdsong fills the space, but as I take a step forward it stops. *Huh*, apparently I don't make a noise when I transport.

I've only been waiting for about five minutes when I hear the sound of a car approaching. It slows to a stop and I hear my name called. I walk out of the tree line and see Xavier's face first. He's sitting in the front seat, still looking tired, but he's got a big smile on his face. "Lookin' for a ride?" he drawls.

Raven laughs from the back seat, and Gregory just shakes his head. "Hey, guys," I say to them.

I hop in the back seat with Raven and she gives me a bright, genuine smile. Seriously, how is she not jaded?

"So what's the plan?" I ask. I'm guessing Mr. Smith left the logistics up to Gregory.

"We're going to drive over to Sariah's house and park a little away from the house," Gregory tells me, "but close enough so you can see the front door. As soon as you see her dad answer it, I want you to transport to her room." His upper body is angled toward me, and one of his hands still has a grip on the steering wheel, causing his forearm to flex. A wave of embarrassment crashes over me as I remember lusting over those muscles, now realizing he heard every single one of those thoughts. Gregory winks at me.

I don't think I'll ever stop dying of embarrassment.

He laughs a little to himself, and Xavier knocks him on the arm. "What's that all about?" Xavier asks, an eyebrow raised.

"Anyways," I say, hoping to change the subject. "Are we far from her house?"

"No, it'll be a quick drive," Gregory says, and faces forward, pulling back onto the road. "Just remember to be as quiet as possible and search everywhere, including her computer. Anything you can find is more than what we have now."

"Aye, aye, captain," I say, giving him a mock salute.

"THERE IT IS," Gregory says, pointing to a beautiful Victorian home. The house is a soft blue, with red accents around the roof line and windows. The front porch looks inviting with its rocking chairs and porch swing. The trees in the front have all changed color, and most have lost their leaves, which are now littering the front lawn. The place looks like it could be on the cover of a Southern home décor magazine.

"Wait for the door to open and then get in there. We'll meet you back where we picked you up," Gregory tells me.

"Why don't I just come back to the car?" I ask.

"I don't know how much time we'll be able to give you while we distract Sariah's dad. And we haven't tried you transporting to a moving vehicle, and I don't want to imagine how many things could go wrong with that," Gregory tells me, and his voice is deadly serious. I hadn't even thought about that.

"Back at the creepy school it is, then," I promise.

They exit the car as one, and I feel like there should be theme music playing like on *Law and Order*. I watch their progress up the front steps and pull up the blueprints on my phone that Mr. Smith sent me. The door opens and I close my eyes. Here's hoping I end up in the right room.

SIXTEEN

This is not what I expected from Sariah's room. Then again, I'm not really sure what I thought I'd find, but the bright yellow walls and insane amount of pictures were not on my list. I probably watch too much television, because this is like a typical nineteen-year-old's room, not the serial-killer lair I was thinking I'd find. I mean, she's not a serial killer, but she is a seriously pissy person; she let Tony get shot, and she helped kidnap a kid. If the shoe fits and all of that.

I step forward and take a closer look at the photos lining the walls. She looks happy in them. But she also seems to be a couple years younger. These have to be from before her mom died. I scan them, and sure enough the next picture confirms that. Sariah stands next to a woman who could be her twin, only twenty years older. Their heads are thrown back in laughter. And it's genuine, not the staged kind you see so much. Her mom's death seriously changed her, but why so drastic? Mine died, but I'm not kidnapping people or having them shot.

There has to be something more here to help us answer that question.

I move over to her desk on silent feet. I don't know if they've moved from the front porch into the house, but I'm not going to chance it.

A Mac takes up a chunk of the desk. I tap the screen, hoping she's like me and never actually shuts down her computer. If it needs a password, I'm totally screwed, because computer hacking is definitely not on my list of skills. With any luck she's lazy like most of us and left it blank so I can just hit enter and be good to go.

As the computer wakes up, I slowly open the desk drawers. Stacks of pictures, pens, Post-it notes, and notebooks are crammed into every available space. I pull out the notebooks.

Not notebooks. Journals. It kind of feels wrong looking at these. But maybe they'll give us something we can work with. And I'm going to keep telling myself that to ease some of the guilt. I thumb through the pages and stop towards the end. All these entries are from almost a year ago.

November 3rd

I can't even be in the same room as my dad right now. He just sits there, staring at nothing. Why isn't he freaking out? Why isn't he demanding answers? Why don't we have a body to even bury? If it wasn't for me getting my powers, we wouldn't even know she died. Did she suffer? Was she captured? Where is my mom? And why did I have to lose my dad too?

Wow, I can't even imagine not even being able to have a real funeral. I turn the page and see three more entries are left in the journal.

December 7th

A postcard came today from Australia. So that's where she was. It kills me to see her handwriting, to see her mention graduation. But the oddest part is her mentioning making another stop on the way home. Where was she heading? I showed my dad the postcard, and all he did was shut himself in his room.

I can't believe I'm thinking this, but I'm starting to feel bad for Sariah. But that stops as soon as Tony's face pops in my mind. She's not the only one who went through hell. All of us at Project Lightning have lost a parent. At least she has one parent left.

December 10th

They came to the house today. They told me it was to help me learn my power, but I know it was to recruit me. I'd rather not go, but it's not like I really have a choice in the matter, especially if I want to find out what happened to my mom. Dad's still like a ghost. At least he's showering now.

Did they promise to find her mom if she joined? I wonder who recruited her. Was it Gregory and Ania that came to her like they came to me?

January 2nd

He came to see me again. I can't believe I let him talk me into going back to that place. Their lies make my skin crawl. Why can't they tell me what happened to my mom? At least he's promised to find out what happened. It's better than the rest have done.

Raised voices jar me out of reading the diary. Time to leave, but I've barely had time to search the computer. I click on her icon and thank goodness there isn't a password. I pull the blank USB out of my pocket and plug it in. I drag the whole desktop over to copy it. Here's hoping it will.

While it's downloading I pull up the internet and look at the search history. Nothing really stands out. She was looking up stuff in Australia, but she got that postcard from there, so I'm not surprised.

Something crashes downstairs. What is going on down there? I thought this was just supposed to be a talk with her dad.

I grab the notebooks and check the download. Seventy-five percent. Come on. Come on.

I look back up at the screen and something catches my eye. She was looking at plane tickets. RGN? What airport is that?

Footsteps pound on the stairs. Time to go. Now.

I rip the USB out with shaking hands. I don't even bother to check if it reached a hundred percent.

They're getting closer, and the hair on my arms stands at attention. I squeeze my eyes tight and picture the haunted, abandoned school.

Wind brushes my face and I open my eyes. I drag a hand across my face. That was too close. I set the stack of notebooks down and then pull out my phone. A text from Xavier pops up.

X: We just left. Be there in five.

Me: Hurry up. This place is creepy.

X: It can't be that bad.

I look around at what essentially is a haunted forest. Yeah, it *can* be that bad.

Me: I'm waiting for one of those ghost hunting show crews to walk by.

X: I wouldn't worry about that.

Me: Why?

X: It's daylight out. They only film at night.

I can picture him saying that, and I know he's being totally serious.

Me: Thanks for that.

X: Anytime.

Me: But seriously. This place is why urban legends exist.

X: Rescue you in just a minute, we're around the corner.

I walk out from the tree line, hugging the notebooks. A car slows as it passes and I wave at the three guys in it. But they stare back at me with horror-stricken faces. I whip around, terrified of what's behind me, but there's nothing there. I turn back and they're pointing and yelling something I can't make out. Is it me? I look down at my clothes, but everything seems fine. I walk towards them and the driver slams on the gas and they take off. Weird.

Gregory's rental pulls up at the curb, so I walk over to it. His eyes meet mine as I get closer. A small smile tugs at his lips and I answer with one of my own as I rush over. Xavier opens the back door, beck-oning for me.

"Hey, do I look weird or something? Or is there stuff on my face?" I ask as I slide into the back seat.

Xavier scans my face and body. "No, everything looks fine. Why?"

I gesture to the street ahead of us. "These guys just drove by and looked totally freaked out by me."

He looks back to where I was just standing and then at notebooks on my lap. He shakes his head and lets out a gruff laugh that sounds like he's got marbles lining his throat.

"What?" I ask.

He motions to my body and the notebooks in my arms. "You're standing there, holding notebooks, in the trees, right next to a haunted school. Do the math," he says.

Raven and Gregory start laughing in the front seat. "You just became a part of a conspiracy theory," Raven says between chuckles.

"I always knew I'd be famous," I say in a deadpan voice.

Everyone keeps laughing, which feels like such a great stress relief, but it's quickly cut off by Gregory's phone ringing. We're still parked on the side of the road, but I think with this conversation, it's needed. Because as the phone rings again, the anxiety just increases tenfold.

Gregory lifts his phone to his ear. He doesn't even say hello, just "Yes, sir," and presses something on the dash.

"Can everyone hear me?" Mr. Smith's commanding voice comes through the speakers.

"Yes," we say in unison.

"Good. Gregory, give me your report," Mr. Smith says.

"Mr. Lewis greeted us warily at first. He thought we were coming to tell him Sariah had died. But as soon as I asked him if he'd heard from her, things went south from there," Gregory says. I feel bad for this poor guy, thinking that he'd now lost his daughter on top of already losing his wife.

Mr. Smith exhales loudly into the phone. "Go on."

"He demanded to know what happened to her," Gregory tells him.

"And what did you say?" Mr. Smith asks.

"I kept to the plan you set earlier. I told him that she took off and we were worried about her. Asked if she had come home. He then accused me of lying, kind of got belligerent after that. He picked up a vase on the table and threw it at the wall." Gregory answers. Guess that's what the crash was, but I'm not surprised by how her dad reacted.

"All right, I didn't really think Sariah had returned home, but you never know. We'll talk more about what you picked up from his mind when you get back. Now, did you all get into the house?" he asks.

"Yes," we say.

"Xavier, what did you find?" Mr. Smith asks.

He leans forward in his seat, hands on his knees. "We didn't get past the front entryway, but luckily that's at least where the mail slot is. He got a letter from Myanmar, but he didn't open it there. Does he have any business dealings in that part of the world?"

"He could," Mr. Smith says.

I clear my throat loudly and everyone turns to look at me. "Who's that?" Mr. Smith asks.

"It's me, Becca."

"Find something?" he asks.

I nod my head, even though he can't see me. "A lot actually, but does the airport code RGN mean anything to you?"

Silence stretches across the line. "Did he hang up?" I whisper the question to Xavier, and he shrugs.

"No, I'm still here," his voice booms across the speakers, making me jump. "I just looked up that code. It's for the airport at Mingaladon, in Myanmar." The air in the car seems to still. "Where did you see that?" he asks.

Adrenaline starts coursing through me. Could this be our break? "Sariah was searching it on her computer."

"What else did you find?" Mr. Smith asks.

"I've got her journals," I tell him. Raven's eyes widen and I hear Xavier mutter a curse. "I'm pretty sure she was meeting with someone from Project Lightning. She's angry. It sounds like she only agreed to join because she wanted to know what happened to her mom. She wants to give her mom a proper burial, to say goodbye." The car gets quiet at my last statement, because we all get it.

"All right, here's the plan. Everyone return to headquarters. I'm going to contact the CIA and see if they can run their facial recognition for the airport and surrounding ones," he tells us. "Hopefully more information will pop up. But with the holiday coming up, I'm not sure. We'll talk more when you guys get here." He hangs up without saying goodbye. I stay in my seat, because he didn't tell me to transport back and I have no desire to return to headquarters alone again.

"Holiday?" I ask as Gregory puts the car in drive.

"Thanksgiving is in two days," Raven tells me.

"Seriously?" I ask, slumping back into my seat, because sadly I had no clue. "This transporting all around the world is throwing me off. Plus it's exhausting." I'm not as tired as I was when I transported across the globe, but I could totally close my eyes right now.

"Are you finding yourself sleeping more?" Gregory asks, his eyes trained on the road.

"Yeah," I say, baffled, because I never noticed it before. "Is that normal when you use your powers?"

Everyone else in the car seems to have some unspoken conversation with one another. "What?" I ask, because clearly I'm out of the loop.

"It's not the norm," Gregory tells me. "At least not from just using your powers."

"So why am I getting more tired?" I ask.

"I don't know. But for now, just make sure to get as much rest as you can. It'll be a couple hours before we get back," Gregory says.

Well, that sucks. I lay my head against the window.

"We'll figure it out," Raven says as she pats my arm and gives me a warm smile.

I hope so. Because I feel like there's this ticking clock inside of me; we need to find Tony, and soon.

SEVENTEEN

I follow behind Raven into Mr. Smith's office. Thankfully the trip back was pretty uneventful. But I've got Sariah's journals under my arm and a USB with her hard drive. Hopefully whoever they get to search this thing will find something in there; we need them to.

"I'm glad to see you here, and all in one piece. Xavier, how are the ribs?" Mr. Smith asks.

"They hurt something fierce," Xavier says as he gingerly lowers himself into the chair in front of the desk.

"After this meeting, head to the medical center," Mr. Smith tells him, and Xavier nods his head. "Good. Becca, what do you have for us?"

I place the journals and USB on his desk. "I'm pretty sure I got the hard drive copied, but I could hear her dad getting close to her room, so I had to leave real quick."

"Whatever you got is better than what we had before," Mr. Smith says. He runs an agitated hand through his hair. "I'm not going to lie. We don't have a lot to go on. And with Sariah having help from within Project Lightning, it's making things especially difficult. I've had to use outside contacts since we have no idea where the mole is. But with Gregory back, maybe we'll be able to find them.

"Here's the plan. Becca, go home for the holiday." Mr. Smith says, completely serious.

"What? I can't leave. I've got to help you," I say, my breathing starting to become frantic.

"You're literally a second away," Mr. Smith says, and when I open my mouth he waves me off. "These past several days have been a lot. More than any of these guys had to take on when they first joined. Go spend time with your grandparents. I need to make sure you've got the right mental framework going on."

I'm furious. My face may be set in a careful neutral mask, but on the inside I'm seconds from erupting. "I'm not a child. I can handle this," I tell all of them.

"Honey, you technically still are," Raven tells me, and I know she's trying to be sensitive, but it's like she lit the match to the powder keg inside me.

"I stopped being a kid the minute my mom died. I stopped being a kid when Ania died and when Tony got kidnapped. Childhood left swiftly and with a middle finger in the air." My pulse pounds in my ears like a sledgehammer. And it takes everything in me not to lash out at Mr. Smith as he opens his mouth.

"We're not saying what you've been through hasn't changed you. What we're trying to say is that, this world is still new," Mr. Smith says. "And if you don't decompress, you won't be able to help us find Tony. It's only for two days. If we have any news, we'll call you and get you back." I hate that he's being gentle with me. Because he's not a gentle man and I'm not made of glass.

I'm starting to open my mouth when Gregory cuts me off with a soft plea. "Please, Becca."

I deflate at the pleading in his voice. "Fine, but you call me right away." I point my finger at Mr. Smith, like I've got some sort of authority.

"We will," he promises me.

"Are you guys going to be looking at Sariah's—"

"Rebecca," Mr. Smith's stern voice cuts me off.

Got it, they want me out of here.

I take a moment to look at each of them in the eye to say goodbye without using words. And I try not to linger on Gregory, because that's the last thing I want Mr. Smith harping about. I close my eyes. To Grandpa's house I go, I guess.

GRANDMA SQUEALS and drops the dish in her hand. It shatters on impact. Maybe I shouldn't have transported into the kitchen, but I wasn't really thinking. I rush over and crouch to the tile floor, picking up the big pieces of ceramic. "Sorry," I tell her.

Her hand is still clutching her chest. "I don't think I'll ever get used to that," she tells me.

"Next time I'll transport to my room or the front door," I promise her.

She takes a deep breath and then joins me on the floor to clean up the plate. "So what brings you home again?" she asks.

I get up and dump the pieces into the trash then grab the broom and dust pan. "They're letting me come home for Thanksgiving," I tell her as I start to sweep up the mess.

She throws out her trash, and Grandpa shouts from down the hall. "You okay, Mae?"

"It's because of me," I yell back to him.

He walks into the kitchen, his eyes looking at the dustpan full of ceramic shards. "Almost gave Grandma a heart attack," I tell him.

I dump the pan into the trash and walk into his arms. He holds me for a long time. "How you doing, kiddo?" he asks softly into my ear. And I know he's really asking if I'm still as bad as the last time he saw me.

"I'm okay," I tell him, and that's a straight-up lie. But I won't burden him right now, especially in front of Grandma.

He steps back but still keeps his hands on my upper arms. "So what's the reason for the visit?" he asks.

"We get her for Thanksgiving. Isn't that great?" Grandma asks, clasping her hands to her chest, the smile on her face beaming.

"Wonderful," he says, giving me one last squeeze before he releases me.

I give him a genuine smile. I hate to think it, but Mr. Smith was right. Being home for only a few minutes has already relaxed me. "Well, I've got some last-minute shopping to do," Grandma says as she washes her hands off in the sink. "We weren't really going to have a whole Thanksgiving, but with you home, we need to now."

Part of me wants to tell her not to bother, but I know it'd be useless. "Do you want to come with me?" Grandma asks, but I know she's just being nice. Woman loves grocery shopping, so I'll stay out of her hair.

"Nah, I'll stay here and keep Grandpa company," I tell her. She walks over and gives my cheek a soft pat.

Grandpa and I watch her leave out the kitchen door and he turns back to me. "Why are you really home?" he asks.

I shuffle over to the kitchen table and plop down into a chair. "Mr. Smith told me to come home for the holiday. With how things have been going, he basically wanted me to come home and unwind," I tell him.

He nods his head. "That's a good idea," he says.

I lift my hands in a helpless gesture, because I really didn't get a say in it, but I'm here now.

"Anything you want to do now?" he asks.

"Take a nap," I tell him.

He rubs my shoulder. "Come find me when you wake up."

I nod my head and go up the stairs to my room. When I walk in I don't know what I'm expecting, but everything is where I left it. Grandma must have been in here though, because there are no clothes in the bin or dust on top of my dresser. My body relaxes even more. Who knew coming to my own room would help?

I sit down at my desk and look at the pictures on the wall above it. Sariah's not the only one who's got photos on her wall from happier times. Except I'm not standing with my mom in any of them. But there are photos of my grandparents and friends.

I wonder if any of my friends are curious about where I disappeared to. I basically cut ties with them, but I thought at least one of them would call here looking for me. The oddest thing is that I feel closer to the people at Project Lightning than I ever did with some of my friends that I've known for years. Maybe I let the feeling of being different hold me back somehow from my old friends. But it's that differentness in all of us at Project Lightning that connects us.

I get up and head for my bed. I wasn't lying when I told Grandpa that I wanted a nap. I transported a lot today, and it's taken its toll.

I plop down and my head hits the pillow. As usual, sleep comes swiftly, but I'm not sure that's always a good thing.

EIGHTEEN

W ell, I'm no longer having these dreams by the water, but from what I can tell from the stump I'm sitting on, this forest around me isn't normal. It almost seems like I'm in a jungle, but I don't think I've ever been to a jungle. So I'm just going to assume what they show on TV shows about jungles is right. It's eerily silent though. I thought a jungle would be teeming with noise. I look around at the bright green foliage, but what I'm really searching for is my mom. Usually in these dreams she's here right when it starts.

"Mom?" I call out. I don't know how long I've been sitting here, but she should have been here by now.

Nothing answers me but more silence. I've never gone exploring in a dream before, but there's a first time for everything. I get up and head to my right. The second I leave the clearing I'm inundated with all sorts of plants. Vines wrap around the trees and drape on the forest floor. Ferns half my height flank the small path I'm following. I look above at the thick canopy, and sunlight is sprinkled about. I follow the small game trail, totally expecting to see some form of life, but there's nothing.

After about ten minutes of walking, I stumble upon another clearing. My mom's back is to me. I walk up beside her. "Didn't know I'd have to traipse through a jungle this time," I say, but she doesn't answer me.

"Mom?" I step in front of her to see her face. Tears are streaming down her cheeks. "Hey, what's with the tears?" I ask.

She points in front of her and I follow where her finger is indicating. Out of nowhere a village appears. Homes that don't look like they belong in a jungle line dirt roads. But I'm still not getting why she's crying.

"He would have loved it here," she says, but I'm not really sure she's talking to me.

I look back at the houses, hoping to see who she's talking about, but it's just us as usual. "Who?" I ask, not really expecting a straight answer.

"Your dad," she responds, and I'm floored. We've never talked about him. What's changed?

"Why here?" I ask, because I feel like we're in a specific place.

She turns to answer me, but a violent storm hits out of nowhere and she's ripped away from me.

"Mom!" Before I can even finish screaming her name, she's gone. Wind and rain lash at me. Why am I not waking up? Lightning strikes the tree next to me. Tree branches explode, causing shards of wood to rain down on me. I drop to the ground and cover my head with my arms, but I can still feel the slices on my skin.

You're not supposed to feel pain in dreams, right? More bolts of lightning strike, and it's like being surrounded by exploding bombs. I stay crouched in my ball, accumulating more cuts to my skin. My heart beats like it's going to come out of my chest. "Wake up." I chant the words over and over to myself.

I hear another boom super close to me, and soon I'm filled with white-hot pain. So much pain that everything turns to black.

MY BODY JERKS upright in my bed. A blinding headache pounds against my temples. *What the hell was that?* I swing my legs over the side of the bed and sit with my head in my hands for a minute. My hair brushes my arm and I wince. I slowly bring my head up and look at my arms. Tiny red slashes crisscross up my arm.

No. Way.

I stumble off the bed, my eyes still focused on my arms, and head for the bathroom. I flip the light on. The cuts are fading from an angry red to a soft pink. How is this even possible? I catch something white from the corner of my eye. I look up at the mirror and almost fall to the floor, but I grip on to the sink to stay upright. There's a white streak in my hair like Rogue's from freaking *X-Men*. How the heck am I going to explain that one? But it starts to slowly change back to its normal dishwater blonde.

I stay staring at the mirror, trying to convince myself that the marks on my arm were real. But it's hard to do that when everything fades back to normal. When I see my mom in another dream, she's got a lot to explain, because I don't think these are just dreams. They are way more. And now I'm terrified of them.

"GRANDPA?" I call out as I get to the bottom of the stairs. I'm still looking at my arms, searching for the marks from earlier, but they're completely gone. I haven't told Grandpa about my dreams; he's already worried about me. Last thing I need to do is add to it.

"In here," he says in a tight voice from the living room.

I walk into the room slowly because of that tightness in his voice, and see Grandpa standing next to the chair facing the fireplace. It's occupied. The only thing visible is the hand resting casually the arm of it. It's just a hand, but the coarse dark hair and large knuckles scream *man*. Grandpa steps forward and extends his hand, and the man in the chair slowly stands. His broad shoulders are covered in a tightly stretched black shirt. His dark brown hair is cropped close to his head. He pats Grandpa on the shoulder.

"Becca," Grandpa says and beckons me closer.

As the other man turns and looks at me, I see his face and my body locks, the air leaving my lungs on a wheeze. It's not often you get to look into the face of a dead man, especially when it's your own father.

"How?" I whisper. My body wants to flee the room and take a step closer all at the same time.

My eyes stay locked on the face I've only seen in pictures. Even if that face has aged, it's still the same. I feel my hands start to shake, and tears gather at the corners of my eyes. I lean against the wall.

"Hello, Becca." His voice is like a wrecking ball to the dam that was holding back my emotions.

"Dad?" I sob.

His eyes drop to the floor for a moment, until he looks back at me with a haunted expression. "No. Your uncle Tiberius, your dad's twin." His voice hints at an accent, but I can't place it.

More like Dad's *identical* twin. My stomach muscles loosen a little; didn't know I was scrunching them. It's eerie looking at him. But I've got an uncle?

I look between him and Grandpa. "Why haven't I met you before? Where have you been?" I ask.

He turns back to my Grandpa. "You want to answer the first question, Joe?"

Grandpa's body sags. "Let's sit." He motions towards the couch across from the chair my *uncle* just occupied.

We walk over and his eyes stay focused on the picture on the mantle of my dad. "I should have told you about him a long time ago." Grandpa looks at me, swallowing thickly. "But you already had so much on your plate with your dad not being here, and then with your mom. I couldn't imagine adding more."

I reach over and grip his hand in mine, giving it a small squeeze. He squeezes back. "Your grandma tried for years to get pregnant, but after several miscarriages, we knew she wouldn't be able to have children. I had work in Russia that was going to require me to be there for some time, so Grandma came with me.

"She heard about an orphanage near where we were staying, and went to visit. Your dad was there, only a few days old. Your grandma fell in love instantly. She went to the orphanage every day to hold him. Working for the government helped with some of the red tape, and after a few months he was ours.

"When my assignment was up in Russia, we brought him home, and since we had been gone for so long, no one questioned whether or not he was ours. We never told anyone he was adopted. We didn't know he had a brother, let alone that he was a twin, until years later."

I knew they adopted my dad. That was never kept from me. But how could they leave out the fact he had a twin? Does Grandma know? And I wonder if she's seen him. I seriously hope she hasn't, because I can't imagine how much that would break her heart. You're looking at what your son should be now, but that knife has to constantly cut through you, because it'll never be him.

I let myself study Tiberius, and it steals my breath again. But this new information is something only he can fill me in on.

Tiberius looks me square in the eye. "Our mom gave us up at birth to a convent, and the nuns didn't know who our dad was. She left a letter for us, but Joe didn't know about it. I think the nuns were afraid that if your grandparents read it, they wouldn't want to adopt your dad. And those nuns knew."

"Knew what?" I ask. My eyes drift to Grandpa, and he's rubbing the back of his neck.

Tiberius takes a deep breath, bracing for whatever he's going to tell me. "Your mom isn't the only one you inherited powers from."

Whoa, *what?* I cock my head to the side, because I'm pretty sure I didn't hear him right. But he just nods his head like he knows I'm doubting my ears. "But how? Dad worked at Project Lightning. They would have never allowed my parents to have me, or even get married. That's like their huge rule, and they *will not* relax on that. Trust me."

Tiberius leans forward, his hands clasped between his knees. "They didn't know about your dad's power. He didn't even know about it until I found him when we were twenty. It took him a while to believe me. He hadn't started working with Project Lightning yet."

"Mr. Smith would know; anyone who touched him would know."

His eyes drift towards the mantle. "Have you ever looked closely at photos of your dad from the last years of his life?"

Where's he going with this?

"He always wore gloves. During his last military operation, he suffered horrific burns on his hands and arms. The nerve damage was at times unbearable. He always wore gloves and long sleeves. People knew not to touch him. And it helped in shielding what he was. Now, if he hadn't died so young, someone would have found out. It was inevitable. Your mom knew obviously, as well as me, but no one else."

I can't focus on his power yet. I don't know why, but it's like my brain refuses to think about it, and instead picks up another fact. "When did you inherit?"

"When we were twenty," he tells me.

"Both of you?" I ask, because if I'm doing the math in my head correctly, that makes more than a hundred.

"Yes, and my telling you this is dangerous. Because I shouldn't exist. I'm assuming they thought my mom terminated the pregnancy or lost the child; never mind that she was pregnant with twins."

"And how did you even find my dad?"

"Because of my gift," he says, and for some reason I find it odd he calls it a gift. I've never heard anyone else call it that. Lately it's felt like a curse.

I look at him, waiting for him to expound on his power.

"I can find anyone like us in the world. It's like there's a map in my mind. And anyone with powers shines like a star on that map. If I've met them, I can find them specifically, but if not, I can just see where in the world people with powers are."

Hope like I've never known blooms in my chest. He can find Tony. But I squash that hope real quick, because I don't know this guy at all. I mean, there are some of the one hundred that hunt the others. I almost got abducted by those two guys, Thompson and Henderson. I'm not going to let that happen again if that's what Tiberius tries to do. He may be my dad's identical twin, but I'm not willing to take the chance and trust him. "Why aren't you with Project Lightning?"

"My mom warned me against it, in the letter she left us. And I met a woman, whom I stumbled upon in Russia. She was like us, and she told me the best thing that I could do was to never reveal myself."

"Then why are you here *now*?" If this woman told him to hide, what made him show up now? And where has he been all these years?

"Walter called me," he tells me, like it's the most natural thing in the world. Grandpa grabs my hand. He knows this is big.

"Ania's dad? How?" How the heck would he know Walter if he hasn't been a part of Project Lightning?

"The woman I met, her name was Magdalena. Walter's wife."

Sometimes I feel like life's coincidences are too many.

"Did you know Ania?" Because if Ania met my dad's twin and didn't tell me...

"No. I never had the pleasure of meeting her."

The relief is instant. I don't think I could handle knowing that another person kept huge secrets from me. And he seems honest in this regard, so I'm just going to go with my gut on this one and believe him.

"Why would Walter contact you?" I ask, because I'm not seeing the connection. Granted, there's a lot about Walter I don't know, and his wife might have told him about meeting this guy, but what is Tiberius going to do for him and Bronia?

"You told him to disappear," he answers. "And that's something I'm very good at."

"He's safe?" I ask him. The guilt over forgetting the phone number he told me to remember still sits heavy on my shoulders.

He nods his head, and the relief is immense. That's one thing I won't have to worry about anymore.

Tiberius's phone dings in his pocket and he pulls it out. I stare over at Grandpa; his eyes are as wide as mine must be. This is the craziest visit. But really, why am I surprised? It's not like there has been any normalcy since my mom died. I don't know why I thought this would be a quiet trip home for Thanksgiving.

Tiberius stands, and it causes me and Grandpa to get out of our seats.

"I'm sorry. I know this is awful timing, but I have to go. Becca, I know you've got more questions. When you're ready, come visit me in Itaituba, Brazil. There's a place right on the river called Beira do Rio. It's a nice little restaurant. Ask for me there, and they'll contact me," he tells me, and I'm floored. Guy just dropped a bombshell and now he's fleeing. Stupid life that's totally like a Lifetime movie sometimes.

I follow him to the door, kind of at a loss of what to say. I mean, what do you say to your long-lost uncle you met like fifteen minutes ago who is now walking out the door?

He turns to me at the front door and pulls a hat out of his bag—a bag I didn't even know he was carrying—and puts it on. As soon as it touches his head, his face contorts and it's like looking at a totally different person.

I take a step back into Grandpa and he grabs my arms. "What—" I point at his face.

"Awesome technology, huh? There's no way Mr. Smith isn't having this house watched. If I want to leave without being followed, this is what I have to do. There's someone in Brazil who makes some crazy things with facial recognition." Grandpa and I stare at him, because I thought things like that existed only on the Sci-fi Channel.

"Come see me soon, Becca," Tiberius says, and then he walks out the front door.

"Smile," Grandpa says quickly, squeezing my arm.

I automatically comply. We stand at the open front door waving and smiling as Tiberius walks away. Like this wasn't the weirdest thing in the world.

As soon as he gets in his car, Grandpa shuts the door. "Did that really just happen?" I ask, still staring at the door.

"I think so?" he says, almost like he's unsure himself.

Crap. I put my face in my hands. "I didn't ask him about Dad's power."

"I have a feeling you're going to see him sooner rather than later. And you know where to find him."

"How long have you known about Dad having a power?" I ask.

"He never told me. I should have figured it out; he left so many clues. But I never pieced it together until now."

I turn and look him square in the eye. "Do you trust Tiberius?" I ask.

Grandpa clasps his hand with mine and walks us back to the living room. He sits down on the couch and I take a cautious seat next to him. He stares at the picture of my father on the mantel. His body is still slumped when he turns to me. "I don't know, but you might need him some day."

NINETEEN

It doesn't feel right being home when we haven't found Tony yet. Thanksgiving is supposed to be all about friends and family, traditions, lots of food, and happiness. But there's this cloud hanging over everything.

At night I sometimes dream of him being alone and scared. I just wish there was a sign, or even a ransom demand. But it's been complete silence. And it's not like I can just transport somewhere and search for him. The world is too big and I'm just one person. Maybe some of the things we found at Sariah's will help. Or maybe she'll be dumb enough to call her dad. She has to know we're searching for her, but it's only a matter of time before she messes up.

Now I'm just itching to get back. I tried so hard on Thanksgiving to be happy, for my grandma's sake, but my mind was elsewhere, and I'm pretty sure she knew. For sure Grandpa knew; he would give me sympathy looks and tell me to keep up the faith. When I get back in the morning, if we still have no leads, I might need to take up Tiberius on his offer. But I don't want the others to know. If Walter called him to disappear, then I can't blow that for him. How am I going to keep this from Gregory though? He's texted me a few times since I've been here, but it's been one-word responses on my end.

I lie back in my bed and, probably for the thousandth time, think about what Tiberius told me. What is my dad's power? Apparently I've had it all along, but there's nothing that's pointing to what it could be. Maybe it's like with my mom's power and I need to learn how to use it.

I've got to get to Brazil. I even went to the library yesterday to look it up on a map. I'm so paranoid that my cell phone and the home computers are being monitored. I swear I'm going to have an ulcer by the time I turn eighteen.

A knock at the door pulls me out of my downward-spiraling thoughts. "Come in," I yell.

Grandpa peeks his head around the door, "Hey, sweets," he says to me, and then walks into the room, shutting the door behind him.

I sit up and put my back to the headboard. "Going out of your mind?" he asks.

I let out a humorless laugh. "Yeah."

He sits down on the edge of my bed, his eyes scanning the pictures on the wall, a small smile stretching across his face. "Why don't you head back tonight?" he asks, turning his gaze back to me.

I sit up a little straighter. "But Grandma wants to have that big breakfast in the morning."

He waves away my comment. "It's okay. We've had you for a couple of days. She might not know what you're doing, but she understands it's important. Just make sure you say goodbye to her before you take off."

I look down at my lap. I want to get back to headquarters. I feel like I shouldn't have left in the first place, but it's been good being here with my grandparents.

"It's okay, kid, I promise she'll be fine with it," he tells me, pushing my foot to get my eyes on him.

"Thanks, Grandpa," I say.

"Thank me by going downstairs and having some pie before you go."

I hop off my bed and follow him down the stairs, finding Grandma standing at the counter, brewing some coffee. She turns as we make our way into the room, her entire face brightening. But whatever she sees makes her smile falter for a moment before she completely wipes it away. "Leaving?" she asks, putting all her focus on the cup of coffee she's making.

"Not before I have another piece of pumpkin pie," I say, and that makes her smile.

We sit at the table and for the next hour we talk about things as if I'm not going to go walk into a dangerous situation as soon as I leave. Grandma reminisces about our trip to San Diego when I was eight. And Grandpa talks about the time I tried to dye my hair red in the seventh grade. It's exactly what I need right now. We laugh so hard I have to wipe the tears from my eyes. It makes it harder to leave, but at the same time it's a good memory I can have to turn to.

I look at the clock and note the time. My grandparents do too. "Time to go?" asks Grandma.

I swallow the ball of emotions getting stuck in my throat. "Yeah," I tell her, somewhat reluctantly, and I realize how much so. It's like me leaving home has brought us closer together. Now when I'm here, I feel her love more than I did when I was growing up. Maybe seeing me follow in my dad's footsteps has made her realize it's not such a bad thing to remind her of him.

She stands up. "You better give me a hug, then," she says softly.

She wraps her arms around me and holds me tightly. I don't know the last time she hugged me like this. "Don't worry, Grandma. I'll be back for Christmas," I promise her.

Her smile is sad, like she doesn't believe she'll see me. But I'll be here with them.

She lets go and walks out of the kitchen. Grandpa comes over to me. The tears start welling in my eyes. Why is this so hard? It's not like I'm not coming back. I bite my lip, trying like hell to stem them, but it's not working. They track down my face and splash onto the tiles below.

His own eyes start to shine, and I throw myself into his arms. If he starts to cry I won't be able to handle it. "If things get bad, you come home. We'll figure it out, whatever it is. But if you're unsafe, I'm always here for you," he tells me, his voice sounding hoarse.

"I will," I say.

"Love you," he says.

"I love you too," I tell him as I back out of his arms. I quickly turn around and transport out of there. I can't hear him tell me goodbye.

EVEN THOUGH I got in last night, I didn't go to Mr. Smith's office. He said Saturday morning, and if I showed early he'd be pissed. So I tried to sleep, but it just didn't happen. And now I'm standing in front of his door. Gregory texted me saying they'd be here in a minute, but I'm way too impatient to wait, so I knock.

His door opens and the man himself is standing there. He looks past me. "I'm early," I say, stating the obvious.

"Come in, then." He steps to the side and motions me into the room.

I quickly walk past him and turn around. "Did you find anything on her computer?" I fire the question off before he even has a chance to close the door.

His body deflates a bit. I don't think I've ever seen him defeated. "Unfortunately, no. The last thing she searched for was that airport in Myanmar, but that was months ago.

"Something did arrive though, and I have a feeling she's connected. A package came extremely early this morning. Xavier should be here any moment. I want him to look it over before we open it." He walks over to his desk and sits down heavily in his chair. I take a closer look at him. His clothes are rumpled and there are black smudges under his eyes.

I can't believe I'm going to ask this, but—"Are you okay?"

My question seems to trigger something, because he sits up and tries to smooth down his wrinkled shirt. "Everything's fine," he says, like my question is ridiculous.

All right then. Last time I do that.

Thankfully there's a loud knock at the door. Xavier walks in without waiting for permission, Raven and Gregory filing in close behind him. Gregory's eyes flare when he sees me, but unless you were looking you'd have missed it.

"Didn't know you were back, Becca. Glad you're here," Xavier says to me, but his eyes are trained on the box close to Mr. Smith. "Is that what you want me to look at?" he asks, pointing at the box.

Mr. Smith grabs the box and pushes it towards the edge of the desk. "This came for Becca this morning. No return address. No identifying labels. Just her name and our postmark," he tells us.

"It's got to be from Sariah, right?" I ask. "Who else would send me a package here? I was just with my grandparents, and I highly doubt they'd send me some serial killer package." I look closely at the box, and thankfully it's small. Because all I can think about is how my roommate two years ago made me watch that old movie *Seven* with Brad Pitt. But this box is way too small to be a head. The mere thought makes me shudder.

"That's what I'm assuming, but let's have Xavier check it out first," Mr. Smith says.

We all crowd around the desk. Xavier picks it up and closes his eyes. His face is blank, but soon his eyes squint and his mouth pulls into a hard line.

"Damn it." He practically spits the words out after a few minutes of complete silence, surprising me. I don't think I've seen him mad yet. "They knew I'd look at this box. Three days ago a postal worker found it in New York. He made some comment about how the package must have fallen off a cart."

His head drops down and his whole body shakes with the deep breaths he's taking. I put a hand on his arm. "Are you sure?" I ask.

His hands grip the box tighter. "Wait." He says the word hesitantly. I keep my hand on his arm, and I know I'm probably squeezing him too tightly, but I don't care. "It's blurry, but I can make out someone placing it in the warehouse." He shakes his head a little and starts breathing like he's out of breath. "I can see their hand. They've got a gold Celtic knot ring on their right ring finger." He drops the box on the desk and his whole body collapses forward. Gregory reaches out and grabs him before Xavier can face-plant on the desk.

I help Gregory maneuver Xavier to a chair and he falls heavily into it. His face is completely drained of color. "Are you all right?" Mr. Smith asks, already around his desk and in front of Xavier.

"I've never been able to go past day three," Xavier tells him between heavy pants. "But they dropped this off right before the three-day mark."

Mr. Smith watches him for a moment, and all our eyes seem to move to the box at the same time. He stands back up and reaches for the box. "The mailroom would have checked this for bomb-making residue before it got to my desk." He says the words, almost as if to assure himself.

He sits on the edge of his desk and then reaches into his pocket, pulling out a pocket knife. We all seem to hold our breath as he slices the tape and opens the flap. I can hear the crinkle of paper, and then he lets out a harsh-sounding breath. He closes the lid, leaving the contents inside, and then rubs the bridge of his nose.

"Well, what is it?" I ask, unable to contain myself.

I hear a thump and I turn to see Gregory's head against the wall, his eyes trained toward the ceiling.

Mr. Smith clears his throat and I look back at him. "In exchange for you, they'll return the missing children and Tony."

"How can you be so sure?" Raven asks.

"By the threat and evidence in the box," Mr. Smith says, avoiding looking at me.

"What's in the box?" I ask, getting closer to the desk.

"That's not important," he tells me.

But it is important. Whatever *it* is could change everything.

I reach out quickly snatching the box from the desk.

"Becca, no!" Gregory shouts, trying to get the box before I can open it, but it's too late and we crash together, sending the box flying through the air. A bloodied, severed finger and a note covered in blood fall to the floor and I dive for the nearest trash can.

"What does it say?" Xavier asks Gregory.

"Tony for Becca," Gregory says in a detached voice.

TWENTY

They need to send me. They need to trade me. I'm not worth the torture that Tony is going through right now. I'm not worth it. I keep repeating that phrase over and over again as I sit slumped next to the door in Mr. Smith's office, my head in my hands. I haven't moved from this spot for the past ten minutes—too afraid to move away from it, really.

"You are too worth it," Gregory says, his voice harsh.

My head whips up and I point a menacing scowl at him. "Stop reading my mind!" I yell back at him.

"I can't help it!" he fires the words right back.

Raven walks in between us. "You two need to calm down so we can think rationally about this," she tries to interject.

"Stop being the peacemaker," I snap back.

She puts her hands up in a helpless gesture. "That's kind of my thing." She says it like it's an apology.

The door opens and Mr. Smith walks back in, followed by Mr. Rivers and Chelsea. Chelsea's eyes narrow a bit when she sees me by the door, but she quickly wipes the look from her face. Whatever, I don't care that I'm sitting on the floor. "Everything okay in here?" Mr.

Smith asks as he reaches his desk, his eyes trained on a very agitated Gregory. Mr. Rivers sits down gingerly in one of the chairs.

"Everything is—" Gregory starts to say but I cut him off.

"Just send me," I blurt out.

Mr. Rivers leans forward in his chair. "You, my dear, are our bargaining chip. The minute we send you, who knows what will happen to those children."

Mr. Smith nods his head in agreement.

"But I can just transport out of there after the kids are released," I tell them, desperately trying to get them to see reason.

"Do you think they'll let those children go?" Mr. Smith asks me. "No. Their powers are too valuable. There are only so many of us left in the world. They won't take a chance of permanently losing any power. And considering who these children belong to, whoever took them won't ever give them back."

"The little girl they have, Sara, one day she'll be able to control water. Can you imagine what that power would be like in the wrong hands? She could cause tsunamis, pull water out of certain areas, causing droughts. The possibilities are endless."

My body collapses back against the wall. "But they'll keep torturing Tony if we don't do what they say," I tell him, my voice cracking.

Mr. Rivers leans forward, resting his chin on top of his hands, which are perched on his cane. "There's a strong possibility. But that's why we're working to find him. And hopefully there is something in that box that will give us a clue. But just like the children, they won't kill him."

I can't just stay here and do nothing. I feel like I need to do something. I go to stand, not really sure what I'm going to do, but Mr. Rivers's voice stops me. "Stay seated." There's something in the tone of his voice that compels me to stay on the floor.

Mr. Smith clears his throat. "While the box and its contents are analyzed, I want you four to go and work with Dexter. Look through all those journals and see if anything sticks out. Dexter will be examining Poppy's clothes and the bag she was in to see if there are any minerals in there." His focus goes back to something on his desk.

"You're dismissed," Mr. Rivers adds, and we all leave the room without question.

Gregory pulls me to the side as soon as the door closes. His arms immediately wrap around me. Xavier rubs my shoulder as he walks by, and Raven gives me a sad smile.

"They cut off his finger," I whisper to him. He tries shushing me, but I just keep talking over him. "Because of me." I press my face into his chest. What's the big deal about me being different from mom?

"You've got to stop thinking about it. We don't even know why it matters that your power is different from your mom. Focus on finding him," he says, holding me tightly.

I shake my head back forth against his chest.

"I need you to be strong," he pleads.

"I'm tired of being strong," I say into his shirt. And I know he can hear the defeat in my voice, but my heart is breaking for my friend.

He takes a deep breath and presses a kiss to the top of my head. I don't think there's anything he can tell me right now to change my thinking. Tony's being tortured because of me, and I don't know how to deal with that.

"Let's go see Dexter and work on finding Tony," Gregory tells me. I nod my head and let him lead me down the hall.

"HEY GUYS," Dex says to us from his spot at a lab table. He gets up from his microscope and walks towards us.

"Hey Dex," I say, my voice lacking any enthusiasm.

Dex looks like he's going to ask me something, but thankfully Xavier steps forward and holds out his hand. "Xavier. We haven't had a chance to meet."

"Oh. Yes, hi," Dex says as he shakes Xavier's hand.

Raven introduces herself as well, and while they all talk with

Gregory, I look over the room. Sariah's journals are stacked on one of the tables, so I head over to them. No time to talk; Tony needs us. I pick up the one on top, have a seat, and dive right in.

December 25th

This is our first Christmas without Mom, and this morning was awful. Dad wouldn't even get out of bed until 10. He tried a little, but nothing was going to salvage today. I want to talk about her. I want to be able to say how much I miss her, but anytime I open my mouth, he begs me to stop. He's not the only one who misses her. But I need my dad to snap out of it right now. He's disappeared, I don't know this guy. And it's pissing me off. I'm so torn between trying to give him a wakeup call, or just packing my stuff and running away. Mom would be so mad if she knew what I was thinking. But he needs to suck it up and be the parent.

"Find anything?" Gregory asks me, his hand on the small of my back.

I blow out a breath and then meet his eyes. "I want to hate her. And I do. Part of me would love nothing more to punch her in the face. But reading these..."

"It makes her like us and not the villain we've painted her as," he says.

"But how does she think kidnapping kids and being a part of Tony's torture will get her information about her mom?" I ask, and I don't know if he can answer that.

"Because she's made choices that have led her down a road she probably never imagined," Raven says as she steps up next to me. "I don't know if she's regretting her choices, or if she's still letting anger cloud her judgment. But the longer she stays on this path, the worse her decisions will be. And her consequences are going to be drastic."

"I get her anger. We all get it. But today..." I can't finish that sentence. I don't want to talk about what was in that box.

"What did Sariah do?" Dex asks from across the room.

"And he doesn't even know about Sariah. No one knows about all the things that are happening." I don't even know who I'm talking to right now, but my mouth has a mind of its own. "Dex doesn't even have a clue about what's going on. You want to know?" I ask Dex, turning to face him.

"Umm, sure?" he looks around at everyone else, super hesitant.

"Becca," Gregory warns.

I wave him way. "No, he's helping us. He should know."

"Let her tell him," Xavier tells Gregory in his gruff, calm voice.

Gregory throws his hands up in the air, so I press on. "Tony's missing. Sariah helped kidnap him and tried to kidnap a little girl. That bag and clothes you're working on"—I point to the pile of fabric in front of him—"that's from Poppy, the little girl from England. But thankfully she's safe now. And today"—my voice cracks—"today we got confirmation that they're torturing Tony." *Because of me.* But I leave those words unsaid.

Dex's face has lost all color, and he looks down at the black fabric in his hand.

Unbidden, my mind fills with unwanted images of what else they could be doing to Tony, and I can't take it. "I've got to get out of here. We're not going to find anything in these journals," I tell them, throwing the one I'm reading down on the table. And I don't bother waiting for anyone's response. I transport right to my room.

I pace in front of my bed. How much time does he have? I can't let him keep getting hurt. How is he even going to come back from this? How are any of us?

I take my cell out of my pocket and drop it on the nightstand, but I keep Mom's coin in there for good luck. I might not be able to find Tony, but I know someone who can.

Tiberius.

TWENTY-ONE

A blanket of humidity covers me almost instantly. Gross. It feels like I just got out of the shower, but I haven't taken one since last night. Thankfully, when I turn, the small, bright-yellow restaurant stands out against the imposing river behind it. This must be Beira do Rio. I head inside and walk up to the counter, where a girl close to my age greets me with a *"Boa tarde."*

"Umm...hi?" What language do they speak in Brazil? Portuguese, right? I don't know Portuguese. I barely know even a few things in Spanish.

"Oh, American?" she asks. Her accent is so heavy I have a hard time understanding her.

"Do you speak English?" I ask, hopeful.

"Yes," she tells me with a big smile on her face.

Immediate relief sweeps me. "Oh, thank goodness."

She laughs a little and it makes me feel even lighter. "What can I help you with?"

I hesitate for a moment, but he told me to come here. "I'm trying to find someone. He said to come here and tell you his name." Man, this feels weird, like straight out of a bad spy movie. "Do you know a man named Tiberius?"

Her face lights up when I say his name. "*Sim!* Yes, yes!"

"Can you get a hold of him, and tell him Becca is here?" My words are urgent, and that seems to change her demeanor.

"*Sim.* I'll be right back." She quickly leaves the counter and heads to the kitchen where a phone hangs on the wall.

I'm not going to even bother eavesdropping, because she's already talking in Portuguese. Instead I look at the menu to distract myself, but I have no idea what any of it says.

She walks back out, a smile still stretched across her face. "He says he'll be here soon."

"All right. Thanks," I tell her. I point to the deck out back, over-looking the river. "I'm just going to hang out here."

She nods, and I leave her to head out to the concrete deck.

The river itself is huge. But what surprises me is how murky and brown it is. It kind of reminds me of the air. Good thing I transported from my room at headquarters, because otherwise I would have had my winter coat on. I walk closer to the metal railing, leaning over it to scan the waterway below. A large barge is far downriver, but up close are a few fishing boats. Men are yelling in Portuguese while they work on nets.

A small boat speeds through the water towards me, but it's still quite a distance off. As it gets closer a man stands at the back control-ling the motor while a woman sits in the middle, her curly red hair blowing in the wind. As they get nearer their faces become clearer. Tiberius. But who's the woman with him?

I stay leaning on the railing as they dock below. The woman gives me a cheery wave; I give her an awkward half-wave, half-salute. She must know who I am. Tiberius's face lights up as we lock gazes.

They hop out of the boat and then disappear for a minute. Voices drift up the cement stairs to my right. Soon they're stepping off the stairs and heading to me. I stand up straight, not having any clue what to do with my hands. Do I cross my arms? Shove them in my pockets? Why am I even worrying about that?

"Becca." Tiberius says my name with warmth.

"Hey there," I say to both of them, but my eyes keep looking to the woman.

He puts his arm around her shoulder and she molds into him. "This is my wife, Lucy."

So I have an aunt.

"Hi," she says, full of smiles.

"I'm happy to see you, but what brings you here?" Tiberius asks, cutting to the chase.

I look around before I speak. "I need your help," I say in a hushed voice. And with those few words, the whole vibe changes. Lucy's smile falls into a worried frown. Tiberius loses all emotion and becomes hyper-focused on my face.

"Did you leave your phone?" he asks.

I nod my head. I know if Project Lightning finds out I'm here, I'll be in serious trouble and I'll put Tiberius in danger. But he's got to help.

He rubs a hand over his face and shares a look with Lucy, one that must come from years of being together.

His eyes connect with mine and he leans into me slightly. "We can't talk here. I'm going to take you somewhere no one knows about. I'm trusting you to keep it unknown," he says, deadly serious.

"I guess we're just going to have to trust each other," I tell him. It doesn't hurt that I can just transport out of the situation. Then again, he could just track me down.

"Let's take a boat ride," he tells me.

WE'VE BEEN TRAVELING for twenty minutes when the small boat pulls up to a dense part of the jungle. We haven't been able to talk over the sound of the motor, but the ride has been tense. I look around for a dock, but I just see young trees lining the shore and other plants that I have no idea what they are.

Tiberius pulls a car remote out of his pocket and presses a button. Just like he was able to change his appearance, the image of the trees parts like a curtain and a small boathouse appears. Where does he get this stuff? Who makes it?

He pulls the boat inside and cuts the engine. Lucy hops out and ties the boat off. "I'm going to head to the house. Give you guys time to talk. Meet you there?" she asks.

"We'll be there soon," Tiberius tells her.

She gives me a wave and a big smile and then takes off.

Tiberius and I both sit in the boat, staring at each other. It still freaks me out to look at my dad's identical twin.

"Let's go for a walk," Tiberius says, and I follow him off the boat.

We leave the boathouse and walk down a dirt road. The farther we go, the thicker the air gets. It feels heavier in my throat, but then again that could just be my nerves. I don't know where we're going or what he's going to tell me, but with every step, I feel my life changing. And that may sound a little dramatic, but my mind keeps telling me to pay close attention.

Sunlight glinting off of metal catches my attention as the trees start to thin out. I stop and stare in awe at the metal-frame buildings hiding amongst the trees. Most are missing a lot of their glass panes from trees and plants having pushed them out. The place has a smell of warm earth and wet leaves. Looking to the right it's like being in the middle of a jungle. But what's really weird is when I turn my head to the left, because it looks like I've stepped into a different time and place—straight into the last dream I had with my mom.

It's such an eerie feeling, but I can't think about it now. I shake my head and force myself to concentrate on what I see now instead of the dream my mind wants to focus on.

There are these random red fire hydrants going down a dirt road. And as I peer through the vegetation, I spot houses that look straight out of suburban America. Granted, it's an America that looks like it got hit by an EMP fifty years ago and has been deserted ever since.

"This place looks like a stage set for a dystopian movie," I say as we walk by a large rusty water tower.

"It may look abandoned, but it's not. Listen," Tiberius tells me.

I humor him, because he's got this mentor vibe going on. We stand there, and at first all I can focus on is the humidity that's making my hair stick to my neck. But then I hear it. Kids laughing. I look around, but I can't find the source. Tiberius points off to our right, and there in the tall grasses, three little kids are running around playing tag.

"Look past the grass," he tells me.

I turn a little more, and I see two women standing off to the side, watching over the kids. I'm assuming they're their moms. I look around and in some of the houses I can see shadows pass by the windows.

"What is this place?" I ask, my voice a lot softer, like if any of these people hear me, they'll scatter.

"Back in the fifties it was founded by Ford and called Fordlandia," he says.

"Like the cars?" I ask, still searching through the trees for more things.

"Yes. They were able to take the local plants and produce rubber. So they set up a whole town here to build cars. But it didn't last and they abandoned this place, leaving all of this here. We've been here for the last ten years."

"Who's *we*?" I ask, because I know this has to be why he told me he's trusting me. Whatever he's hiding has to do with this place.

"Those who should not exist," he tells me, his voice sad.

At his words, I turn and stare at the kids he's still watching play, a small smile gracing his face. "Not exist?" I ask.

He turns away from the kids and faces me, his whole demeanor shifting towards a more serious conversation. "You were told there were only a hundred like you in this world. That's a lie."

Wait a minute. I take a step away from him. "What are you talking about?" Mr. Smith told us there were a hundred of us left in the world.

"I told you how my power is being a finder. I find those like us—far more than the hundred they told you about."

I shake my head. "How is that even possible?"

"Lucy, myself and others have spent the last ten years rescuing others—"

"Rescuing?" I ask, cutting him off.

He looks behind us and points to a spot at a nearby tree. "Here, let's go sit and I can tell you some more."

I warily follow him to a super random bench on the dirt road. We both sit down gently, because who knows how long this has been here and when it's going to give way.

"Your dad and I, we're not counted in that hundred. And the majority of the people here aren't either. This all started after your dad died. You know how I found him using my power. I found Lucy that way too."

I had no idea Lucy had powers. But I didn't shake her hand.

"I told you how my power works. I've always known there were more than a hundred. But when I finally found my brother and he told me there were only a limited amount of us, I told him that was wrong. He never got the chance to look into it. And I don't know who at Project Lightning knows the truth."

No wonder he stays hidden. If the traitor found him...

"The day I found Lucy, I was in Florida and almost got into a car accident because I drove by a building and it was like all of these light bulbs went on in my mind. People like me were in that building, and I had to find out why. So I snuck inside and I was horrified at what I found."

I lean forward at those words.

The sound of a child's squeal makes us both freeze, but Tiberius's faces changes instantly. He smiles so brightly at the sound, but then he shakes his head and quickly sobers as he goes back to our conversation.

"There were holding cells; lab equipment was everywhere, and there were these people that looking terrified, beaten, and shackled. And I knew they were like me, but I had no idea what I'd stumbled upon."

"How did you even get in there?" I ask him. Did he like shimmy in an air vent or something?

He waves my question away. "That's a whole other story. Someday I'll talk to you about my life growing up in Russia. But back to what I found. I saw Lucy. She was there, in one of the cages, and when ours eyes connected, I knew I had to get her and the other people out of there. So I did."

He says it like it wasn't a huge operation. But the logistics seem impossible.

"What were they doing to them?" I ask him.

He looks off into the jungle, and I wonder if he's replaying that time in his mind. "They were part of a series of experiments."

Whoa. What?

"DNA manipulation." His voice drops into an incredibly angry tone. "They were taking genetic material from the hundred and forging it with their test subjects." It's the way he says *test subjects* that makes the hair on my arms stand up and my heart race.

I hear those kids' laughter again. And my stomach turns. This is a place for others with powers. Those children were test subjects.

TWENTY-TWO

Tiberius stands up from the bench, blocking my view of the kids playing tag in the tall grass. "I think we should go see Lucy for the rest of the story."

I get up and follow him down a dirt road. Dilapidated craftsman homes line both sides of the street. "This is like where the fifties went to die," I say, looking at what must have been an amazing front porch back in 1950.

He follows my gaze. "It's really a trip, but most of these houses look a lot different on the inside."

"Why not keep up the outside then?" I ask as we pass another house where thick ropes of vines have crept up the walls and attached themselves to the rain gutters.

"If you look closely, it's kind of maintained. We keep it so it's not too overrun, but it makes for good camouflage."

I try and look closely at what he's talking about, but I just see a bunch of plants and dirty buildings. He's right about one thing though; it's a good cover.

We stop in front of a small home, which at one point was probably white, but now it's dirty and has what looks like a water line on the house from flooding. He opens the door and I follow him in, but as soon as I walk in the door, I stop at the view in front of me. Beautiful, clean hardwood floors greet me. And the whole room smells like fresh-baked bread, which is amazing. It's not a show home, but it's clean and inviting. There are no plants growing in through the windows or floorboards, so that's a plus. And the humidity is nonexistent.

"Ti?" Lucy calls from somewhere near the back of the house.

"It's me and Becca," he tells her.

We walk into a front room and find Lucy sitting at a worktable covered in parts. I don't even know what I'm looking at, but there's a lot of metal and wires. "Hey, baby," he whispers to her as he bends down to kiss her. She tilts her back to give him better access, and that's when I notice she's holding wire cutters.

"How's it going?" she asks, her whole face beaming.

He winces a bit, and I watch her erase any expression on her face. "I was just telling her how we met," he says, his voice soft.

"Ah yes, very normal first meeting," she says, with a heavy dose of sarcasm.

He sits down on the couch next to her and motions for me to have a seat. "Thought it'd be best if we came here and finished the conversation with you," he tells her.

She leans forward and rests her arms on her knees, her hands fisted between them. "It isn't a pretty story," she tells me, and her eyes connect with mine.

I doubt it is, but I need to hear it. I rub my mom's coin in my pocket. I suspect losing my dad wasn't the only reason she turned to drugs. I'll never know now, but maybe with this information I'll understand more.

"I was put into foster care when I was about six years old. After years of some horrible situations, at sixteen I ran away." Her gaze drifts to somewhere over my shoulder, like she's seeing all those horrible times flash before her eyes.

"And being on the streets at that age is scary. After a year of trying to scrape together enough money to live, I met a man that would come into the diner I worked at. And wow." She shakes her head in disbelief. "When you're seventeen and an older, extremely attractive guy shows interest, it's hard not to fall under that spell. I didn't know he was grooming me. I had no clue that he already knew all about me."

She looks down at her hands clasped in her lap, and I scoot farther forward on the couch cushion. "When you've never experienced love from anyone, it's really hard to decipher that someone's undivided attention isn't necessarily love. All I could think was, 'finally, someone to love me, someone to *see* me.' But after six months, everything went to hell."

A harsh laugh slips out of her. "See, I didn't realize that when he came to see me all the time, he was staking a claim on me. He'd pick me up from work, and when he was early he'd talk with my boss. He was also monopolizing my time so much that any friends I had, I stopped talking to. He didn't like my friends, and manipulated me into distancing myself from them. He was slowly isolating me. I was so young and dumb."

I watch her swallow hard, and Tiberius grabs her hand, bringing it into his lap. "I really believed I was going to be with this guy forever. That came crashing down one night when he said we were going to dinner, but then I felt a prick in my arm, like a bee sting. When I woke up, I was in a warehouse, strapped to a bed, and there were other people strapped to tables around me."

My heart starts to race. I know she's sitting in front of me right now, safe, but I can still feel her terror from that time, and it's saturating the room. "The fear that went through me was paralyzing. One minute I'm in a car with a guy I'm convinced I'm in love with, and the next I wake up in hell. The moment that probably broke me though, was when he walked back in. I called his name. Begged him to tell me what was happening, but he looked right through me. Like the months we'd spent together never happened. He talked with some man about payments, and the next woman he was to go after. I didn't realize it until later, but I was just a paycheck."

"What did they do to you?" I ask.

When she looks back up at me, the smiling woman from earlier is gone, and her eyes show how haunted she still is. "They changed me..."

She pulls her hand from Tiberius's, and shakes her hands out a little. "I'm not going to go down that road. You don't need to know everything that was done to me, just that they changed my DNA. They saw me as easily disposable, and I was. No one cared when I disappeared. So they took me as a test subject to see if they could give someone powers."

"And did they?" I ask.

"You've seen the technology that Tiberius uses?" I nod my head. "I'm not sure if anyone had or has a power like this. But before, I couldn't even do basic algebra. Now I'm able to create all these things. It's like these blueprints just appear in my mind."

So she's the one behind Tiberius's crazy disguise and the other gadgets around here.

"Thankfully, when I found her, they hadn't learned yet what she could do. Most of the time those experiments resulted in disaster. If they had known about Lucy..."

Tiberius lets the words lie, but if she still shows fear ten years later, I don't want to know what her life would be like now.

There's a knock at the door and some shouting in Portuguese.

"That'll be Maria coming to help with the bread that's rising in the kitchen," Lucy says. She rises from the couch and stops in front of me. "I'm sorry we can't talk more. But just know, this place is a safe place. My story is just one of many here. You're always welcome in our home." Her voice is soft but full of meaning.

"She's right. I don't think it's safe for you stay at Project Lightning," he says.

That's probably true, but I need him to know why I can't leave there. I tell him about Tony and Sariah. About our mission. The missing kids. I don't leave anything out.

"I can't leave yet. I've got to help, but right now I need a favor. We've hit a dead end. I don't know what to do." I let the desperation show in my voice. He's our last hope.

"I've never met Tony, so I can't know exactly where in the world he is." My whole body seems to slump at his words.

"But with your help, I should be able to." He says it like I should know exactly what he's talking about.

"My help?" What the hell can I do?

"Your dad's gift," he tells me.

When he was at my grandparents, he never got the chance to tell me what my dad's power was. And to be honest, with everything, it's slipped my mind.

"I know you can do more than your mom, and that's because your dad's power is to enhance. So instead of just running really fast—"

Throw my hands up in the air, cutting him off.

"I can transport," I say. So much makes sense now. Like how Gregory always says he can hear my mind more clearly. Or how Tony could see into space farther. Man, even Xavier being able to see past his three day restriction.

"But how does it work?" I ask, also wondering how I'm going to use this to help.

"I'm assuming, like myself, you had to learn how to manipulate your power to transport. You're going to have to do the same with this. For now, hold my hand," he says, while holding out his.

I look at it for a minute. This is kind of weird, but I'll do it if it'll help find Tony. I place my hand in his. "Do you have any idea where in the world he could be?" he asks.

"The last time I saw Sariah she was in England, but Tony wasn't with her. One of the last things Sariah looked up on her home computer was an airport in Myanmar. And that's not too far from North Korea, where he was taken." Really I have no clue where he is.

"Okay. Let's try scanning Asia. I'm not sure if this will work, but it's worth a shot. Close your eyes and think of finding Tony in Asia," he tells me, and he gives my hand a squeeze.

I close my eyes, and I'm probably squeezing his hand too tightly, but I keep an image of Tony's face front and center. We need to find him, and I keep chanting those words over and over in my mind.

"Whoa," Tiberius says, and he drops my hand to grab his head with both of his.

"Did you find him?" I ask.

He starts to list from side to side. "Tiberius? Is this normal?" He's not saying anything.

His arms drop limply to his side. His body sways one more time, and before I have a chance to reach for him, he's falling forward, crashing to the floor.

"Lucy!" I scream.

I drop to my knees on the floor next to him. I shake his shoulder, but he doesn't react. Lucy comes running into the room, an older lady coming in behind her. She rushes over to him and places one hand to his neck, and puts an ear close to his mouth. "He's breathing and his heart is steady," she says, her breathing heavy. "What happened?" she asks me, all her focus on Tiberius.

I shake my head, having no clue. "He was helping me find someone, and he just passed out. Does this always happen?" I ask.

"No," she says, looking as uncertain as I feel. "But he's out, and I have no idea for how long."

I look at the clock again. Too much time has passed. "I've got to go," I tell her, and she looks at me for the first time. "They think I'm in my room." I wring my hands together.

"Did he tell you anything?" she asks. I shake my head no.

"Go. He'll figure out a way to get the information to you." She reaches out and grabs my arm, looking me square in the eye. "Remember, tell no one about this place. It needs to stay a safe haven for those like me."

"I promise," I tell her, and in a blink of an eye I'm back in my room.

TWENTY-THREE

I pace the area between my bed and door. Exhaustion is working me over hard, but there's too much going on and I can't give in to that right now. I've got too many questions that need to be answered, like how's Tiberius going to get the info to me? It's not like he can call me, or call my grandpa either. Should I just transport back there? He could still be knocked out. This is ridiculous. He could know where Tony is. We're so close to finding him. And I can't keep letting him be tortured.

I make another loop, creating a path in the carpet, and then there's a knock on the door. I stop mid-stride. I've got to get myself together. Because if it's Gregory on the other side of that door, he's going to know.

I shake my hands out and bounce a little in place. I can do this. Just focus on thoughts of finding Tony. I walk to the door and open it. Gregory stands there, his eyebrows drawn together.

"It doesn't look like you've calmed down," he says.

I turn and walk back into my room. I hear the door closing as I sit down on my bed. "I'm just stressed," I tell him.

He joins me on my bed, wrapping an arm around me, and I fall into his chest. My head rests right near his heart, and its steady beat helps my heart stop racing. "We'll find him," he promises me again.

I let out a breath. "I know."

We stay there in each other's arms and my body relaxes even more. My eyes start to close a bit, finally giving in to the exhaustion. "I've got something for you," he tells me.

That wakes me up. I sit up, and he digs a hand in to his pocket. "This is for you," Gregory says as he hands me a small black box.

I open it, and nestled in the center of white satin is a pair of earrings. They're mostly made up of this really bright orange stone. I stare at them, because I don't think I've worn anything this bright since I was five.

He laughs a little. "I went and talked with Dexter about the stones that can block mind reading." I perk up at that. "He found some carnelian stones and he amped up the ability in it to block me. I took them to a jeweler, and now here we are."

I lightly touch the earrings, hope surging. "Do you think it'll really work?" I ask.

"Only one way to find out." He taps my ears lightly.

I take the studs in my ears out and then put in the new carnelian ones.

Anything?

Gregory and I just stare at each other. And after a moment it gets a little awkward.

I raise my brows at him.

"Nothing," he says.

A huge smile spreads across my face. "This is amazing," I say.

"Yeah," he says, but his voice sounds off. He's facing me, his eyes are looking at mine, but it's like he's staring off into space.

"You okay?" I ask.

He blinks a few times, and his eyes finally focus on mine. "It's been a really long time since I've been around someone and it's been quiet."

"But that's good, right?" I ask, hesitantly.

He scratches his temple. "It kind of feels like losing a part of myself. But it's also nice not to have to brace myself for the onslaught of thoughts. I don't know if I'm making any sense."

I'm guessing it would be like if I couldn't transport anymore, but... "I think it'll be good for us," I tell him, grabbing his hand.

"Yeah." He doesn't sound so sure, but I am. If we're going to work on being with one another, I need this space. And hopefully in time he'll be okay with it. It's just new.

"Do you think I need to take both out in order for you to hear me?" I ask.

"No clue. Dexter didn't mention that. Try one."

I take out one of the earrings. *So, how 'bout now?*

He squints at me. "There's like a soft whisper. I know this is going to sound weird, but shout at me in your mind."

LIKE THIS?

He laughs hard for a second. "Yeah. I heard you that time loud and clear. But you know it's not going to be convenient for you take your earrings out if you're like tied up and need to talk to me."

I put the earring back in. "I'd just transport out of there. I think the only thing that can stop me from transporting is if I'm unconscious."

He tilts his head to the side. "Actually, that's not true," he tells me.

"How can that not be true?" What else could stop me?

He shifts on the bed a bit and his eyes drift to the door. "There are two people who you wouldn't be able to transport around if they didn't want you to." Is he not allowed to tell me this stuff?

I motion with my hand to continue when he doesn't say anything for a moment.

He rubs the back of his neck. "Have they told you what Mr. Rivers can do yet?"

"Noooo." Now I'm even more intrigued.

He fills his cheeks with air and blows it out in a big puff. "I doubt I'm supposed to tell you this, but I'm going to anyways." He pauses, and the suspense is killing me. I'm mere seconds from kicking him in the shin if he doesn't continue. "He's got the power of suggestion."

My eyes widen. "He can control minds?" I ask, my voice bordering on hysteria.

"Well, kind—"

"How come he's not doing that all the time, then?" I ask, completely interrupting him, but this is some serious stuff.

"I don't—"

"What if Tony really didn't get kidnapped? What if he planted that thought?" Maybe that's why Tiberius passed out. Wait, that doesn't make sense.

He grabs on to one of my arms. "There's—"

"What if we're actually hooked up to some machines like in that movie *The Matrix*? Like this isn't real?" I pinch myself, but it hurts.

"Come—"

The implications of it all! "Is my whole life—"

"Becca!" he grabs my shoulders and gives me a little shake.

"What?" I ask, looking up from the welt I've given myself.

"*The Matrix*? Really?" His face says I'm kind of crazy, but his voice says he thinks I'm kidding.

"What, it's not that crazy. After all, we have powers." And I just saw what Lucy can create, so it's really not that far-fetched.

"You've got a point there. But he wasn't even there when Tony got kidnapped. And he doesn't even have children because he thinks that power should die with him."

"Huh, that's sort of...noble of him." But does he really not have kids? Because Project Lightning is all about keeping the hundred alive.

"What, did you think he was a villain or something?" he asks, his voice sounding like he thinks I'm joking, but worried I'm not.

I give him a look like *duh*. "Well, usually mind control falls in that category."

He shakes his head at my response. "In movies. Plus, it's not mind control, it's the power of suggestion."

"Same thing," I say, tipping my hands like a scale. "And you know what, where else am I going to base my knowledge of people with super powers?" It's not like we learn about them in history class.

I think I've finally exasperated him, because he just lets out a tired laugh. "Back to what I was saying earlier. Besides Mr. Rivers, there's someone out there who can null powers."

I perk right up at that. "Null them? Like you wouldn't be able to use them?" I ask.

He nods his head. "Exactly." Whoa, that's crazy.

"Who?" I ask, because I'm assuming I haven't met them yet. I've always been able to use my power.

"I'm not sure. I picked up Mr. Rivers's thoughts on it once. I just remember him thinking he needed to bring 'her' next time to null things." He frowns, probably mad he has no clue who it is.

"Are you sure he didn't just tell you to think he thought that?" That is a valid question.

But he just shakes his head and throws his hands up. "You're going to ask questions like this all the time now when it comes to Mr. Rivers, aren't you?"

I tilt my head back and forth. "Probably."

"Don't you read Mr. Rivers all the time?" I ask.

"Surprisingly, no. Either he's got some incredible mental shields or maybe he's got some carnelian stored in his pockets." He says it like it still bugs him.

"Isn't Chelsea with him a lot when you're around?" I ask, because I feel like I see her all the time around him.

"Yeah." He draws the word out, like he hasn't really considered it.

"Could it be her?" I ask, because it seems the obvious conclusion.

He scratches his chin. "Maybe, but I've read her mind before. And I think if she was the null, I wouldn't be able to read her."

We fall silent and stare at one another. Gregory reaches his hand out and runs his thumb over my ear. Tingles race up my spine at his slight touch. "It probably would have been better if I got you a necklace, but it's easier for someone to rip that off over earrings."

I touch the other earring, rubbing my finger over the smooth stone. "These are perfect. Thank you."

His hand moves to cup my cheek, his thumb stroking my jaw. He leans closer, but he pauses searching my eyes. "I can't read your mind; I need to know if it's okay to kiss you," he says, looking for permission.

We haven't kissed since before the mission in North Korea, and I haven't let myself think about it too much. But now...I want it.

I lean the rest of the way forward and softly rest my lips against his. I let my hands travel up his arms, onto his shoulders. Our lips lightly brush each other's back and forth. Gregory's hand moves up my neck, into my hair, fisting it lightly. And I turn my head a bit to deepen the kiss. I gently run the tip of my tongue across his bottom lip, and that seems to be a trigger for him, because he lays me down on the bed.

The kiss becomes more frantic, more searching. My heart pounds in my chest and he must feel it, being pressed against me. I turn my head to catch my breath and his lips land against my neck. He kisses his way back up to my lips, but before he can reach them, his phone dings with a message.

He hangs his head. "Damn it." I smile at his words.

He leans down again, but his phone dings again two more times. "It's got to be important," I tell him, completely out of breath.

He leans the rest of the way forward and presses a quick kiss to my lips before he gets up, and I follow suit.

He looks at his phone, scrolling through messages. "Mr. Smith wants me to meet with him in his office, and the rest of you guys to come in about an hour," he tells me, running a hand through his hair, probably trying to fix it.

"I'll see you in an hour," I tell him, trying to fix my shirt. I probably need to fix my hair too.

He leans forward, our lips lightly brushing. "See you soon," he tells me, and heads out the door.

TWENTY-FOUR

My cell dings from its spot on the nightstand. I pick it up. Grandpa texted me?

It was great having you home. Hopefully next time you come back we can go eat at Beira do Rio.

Did Tiberius contact Grandpa? Should I go back to Brazil, or should I go see Grandpa?

I close my eyes and hope Grandpa is the right choice.

I transport into his office to avoid Grandma. He's standing by the window, his cell still in his hand.

"Grandpa," I call.

He turns around quickly and his whole body relaxes when his eyes land on me. "Oh good, I was hoping you'd be that fast," he tells me.

"What do you know?" I ask, walking closer to him.

He gestures to his computer. "I got an email from a friend a few minutes ago," he starts telling me.

"Isn't that dangerous for both of you?" I ask, before he can tell me anything else.

He waves away my question. "Don't worry about us. We both

have ways of hiding correspondence," he says, like it's not a big deal that he's kind of admitting to having spy training.

"What did he say?" I ask.

"He said that Tony's in Myanmar"—I knew it!—"but they're moving him. He thinks it's just between buildings, but they were near the Shwedagon Pagoda in Yangon. That's a pretty heavy tourist area."

I have no clue what he's talking about. "Pagoda?" I ask.

He starts tapping on his cell. "It's the most sacred Buddhist temple in Myanmar. Here," he says, and hands his phone to me.

The best way I can describe the building on the screen is a huge upside-down, golden ice-cream cone. It's a large spire with decorative rings encircling it from top to bottom. In front are at least twenty smaller versions of the larger building. The whole thing shines like a beacon.

"I've never seen that much gold in my life," I tell my grandpa as I hand the phone back to him.

"It's pretty impressive," he says.

"So Tony's somewhere around there?" I ask.

He nods his head. "That's what he saw."

I pace in front of his desk, trying to formulate some kind of plan. "Does he have more? Maybe I should go see him again," I say, because I need an exact location.

"He thought you might say that. He told me to let you know he's going to be traveling real soon. Something about others like Lucy," he says.

Well, that ruins *that* idea. But at least I have a pretty good location to work with. Now if I can just get Xavier and Gregory there.

"How am I going to get everyone there? I can't tell anyone about Tiberius. Sariah *did* look at the airport there." I run through all these scenarios in my mind, but I can't think of anything that won't cause suspicion.

"Use the airport angle. See if they'll let you transport there to look around. And push them to use whatever resources they have to search the area," he tells me.

"I'm going to need to be a good actor," I tell him, and he nods his head.

I close my eyes for a moment and rub my head, trying to get rid of the headache that's building. "I've got to get back. Are you sure you won't get in trouble for any of this?" I ask him.

He waves away my concern. "No one will ever know. Go find your friend, and be safe," he tells me.

I give him a hug, we exchange "I love yous," and I head back to my room.

"YOU'RE KIND OF LOOKING like death warmed over," Mr. Smith tells me as I take up a spot against the wall.

"Thanks?" Geez, way to be subtle.

Xavier leans over. "I think he just means you look tired."

"I am tired," I tell him. I'm exhausted; my body is begging me to sleep for the next ten hours. But I can't tell him it's because I've been to Brazil and my grandparents' and back, all within the last couple hours.

"Where's Raven?" I ask him.

"She's still talking with Dex. He found out she could talk to animals and they went off on a whole thing about seeing if certain animals had information about minerals that humans wouldn't think about. I don't know, but it's the first time she's genuinely smiled in twenty-four hours." Can't fault her for that.

The office door opens, cutting off our conversation, and Gregory walks in. "Sir," he says to Mr. Smith.

"Anything?" Mr. Smith asks.

"Nothing that you guys haven't found already. And nothing that points to a specific person she could be working with at Project Lightning," Gregory tells him, his voice heavy with frustration.

Mr. Smith steeples his fingers in front of his face. "We're going to need you to sit in on interviews," he says.

"Interviews?" I ask, interrupting their conversation. That's going to take forever, and Tony might be out of Myanmar by then. "We need to move on this fast before something else happens to Tony."

"We are. I promise you," Mr. Smith tells me, and turns back to Gregory.

I stand against the wall, listening to the two of them go back and forth about things we've already talked about. They mention the computer again, and I realize that this is it: I just need to sound convincing enough to get them to let me go search there.

"Did you ever check that airport that Sariah was looking up, the one with the code RGN?" I ask, causing them to stop their conversation and look over at me.

"They're doing it now," Mr. Smith tells me.

I step closer to them. "It's the only thing that seems super random to me. I could see if her mom had been there, but she wasn't. And she looked at it after her mom died. So either she knows something about where her mom was going after Australia, or she looked it up after talking to the traitor here. What was her mom doing?" None of this feels like a coincidence, and I need them see that.

The room falls silent at my question.

"I'll have our tech guys look more closely at who's coming and going from that airport," Mr. Smith says, conveniently ignoring my question about Sariah's mom and her last mission.

"You could send me there," I tell him, and I can feel the other guys in the room stare at me, but I ignore them. Specifically, I feel Gregory's eyes boring into the side of my head, probably pissed as he's trying to see where I'm going with this. But I pretend I don't notice. I've never been more grateful that he doesn't know what I'm thinking. I promised Lucy I would keep Fordlandia a secret, and I don't want to go back on that promise or put Gregory in danger for knowing it.

"Myanmar is a big area," Mr. Smith tells me, like this is a ludicrous idea.

I bite my lip, and come up with the quickest thing I can think of. "Yeah, but isn't the airport in a big tourist place? At least when I looked it up it seemed it was. It couldn't hurt to look around; it's the perfect place to hide in plain sight."

"Where would you even look?" Mr. Smith asks, leaning closer to me. He can't be suspicious, can he?

"Tourist areas? I don't know, I just hate sitting here and not doing anything," I tell him, which is true and he knows that. And hopefully he'll take that response at face value.

"Let's see if we find anything else. For now, get out of here, get some dinner and sleep. Hopefully by tomorrow we'll have something," Mr. Smith says, and his eyes are already focused on the papers on his desk.

I start to say something else, but Xavier places a firm but comforting hand on my arm. I look up at him, and he slowly shakes his head. He ushers me out the door, and Gregory follows close behind us.

"You coming with us to eat?" Xavier asks.

"I need sleep," I tell him. My body is close to collapsing right there in the hall.

"You okay?" Gregory asks as he steps up close to me, his hand lightly grazing my hip. And that causes all my nerve ends to fire.

"I'm desperate for some good rest," I tell him. He searches my eyes, and I know it's killing him that he can't tell if that's the truth or not. "I promise, I actually just need to go to bed."

"All right, but don't go transporting off to Myanmar without telling us," he says.

"I don't think I could right now, even if I tried."

He gives my hip a squeeze, and I watch the two of them walk down the hall towards the cafeteria. I turn and head for my room. That's how tired I am, I can't even transport.

TWENTY-FIVE

"Now where are we?" I ask my mom, and I know I sound irritated. But last time we were in Brazil. Now I'm staring at a gate. The sides are two bright pillars, topped in gold, adorned with colorful flags. And I'm pretty sure above the gate, in metal, it says Emperor of India.

She looks at the gate and her face looks as confused as me. "I'm not really sure," she tells me. At least this time she seems more together, because the last dream was like a nightmare. And part of me would rather wake up right now, because I don't want to be struck by lightning again.

"Do you know why we're here?" I ask, eyes still trained on this very colorful gate.

She closes her eyes and takes a deep breath. "What are you trying to find?" she asks.

"Tony." And that's all I say, because I know these dreams are so much more, but I don't know if they're good or bad.

She walks forward, not saying anything, and I follow her. We pass underneath the gate and into an open, vacant courtyard. She points at the wall, "See that?" she asks.

I look from her to the wall and back again. "I just see a bright teal wall."

"Look closer," she says, and it kind of makes me mad. This happens in movies all the time. Why can't the person just walk up to whatever they're looking at and point to it? Why do they make you "look closer"? It seems counterproductive if I'm being honest.

I stare at her until she grows annoyed with me, because I don't want to keep guessing. She lets out a huff and walks to the wall. "See this line?" she asks, and I step up next to her and stare at where her finger is pointing.

"What is that?" I ask. It just looks like a crack in the wall.

"It's actually a seam to a door," she tells me, still pointing at the crack.

"All right, so why are you showing me this?" I ask, because I have no clue where we are or what this has to do with anything.

"Just remember it," she tells me.

"Got it," I tell her. But am I really going to ever see this door in real life? Because let's be honest, most of her advice is cryptic. Like the time she told me they were coming for me, but no one's come for me. I guess she was in Brazil last time, but that dream didn't tell me anything.

"Now, just in case—"

A loud booming rips me out of my dream. I bolt upright in my bed. *What—*

Someone pounds on my door.

I whip off the covers and run to open the door. Xavier stands there, breathing heavily. "They've got something. We've got to hurry back to Mr. Smith."

"You go on ahead, let me put shoes on and I'll transport there," I tell him, and he takes off running down the hall.

I slam the door and scramble to put my shoes on. I grab my phone and my mom's coin from my bedside table. I don't even close my eyes this time, just blink and I'm standing in front of Mr. Smith and Gregory. "What's going on?" I ask.

Both flinch a little at my sudden appearance. "We got a hit off our facial recognition at the airport in Yangon," Mr. Smith says. He turns motions to the holographic image hovering above his desk.

"Who is that?" I ask, because all I see is a white teenage boy with a t-shirt, jeans, blue ballcap, and black frame glasses.

"That's Sariah," Mr. Smith tells me.

"No way." I get closer to the image, but I don't see it.

"Look," Mr. Smith says as he types something into a keyboard. The image changes to a picture of Sariah and the teen boy overlapping. The image shifts to show the identical facial markers on each picture. It's a perfect match. I turn to Gregory and we stare at each other with wide eyes.

"What now?" I ask, ready to go anywhere and do anything.

Xavier comes running through the door with Raven in tow, both of them sucking back lungfuls of air. "These three are hopping on a private jet in a few minutes to head for Yangon. It'll take a good amount of the day to get there. Becca, I need your eyes and ears there. I'll be sending some pictures to your phone of Sariah's disguise and two other people we think are working with her."

He looks at each of us individually before he finally lands on me. "Everyone needs to be in constant contact. Understand?" Mr. Smith asks.

We all nod our heads.

"Good. You three get going. Make sure you sleep on that flight, because as soon as you get there you're hitting the ground running."

They all rush out the room, not bothering to say goodbye, but that's okay because I'd rather have them on that plane.

"Becca, I don't want you transporting all the way back here to sleep or eat, so I've already booked you a room at the Azumaya Lavender Hotel. Your room is under the name Janelle Smith."

"Got it," I tell him, already hopping from one foot to the other.

"Now listen closely," he tells me, and I lean forward at his tone. "You are not to engage with any of them, do you understand? We don't want to spook them. You wait for the rest of the team and we'll proceed from there. Hopefully we'll have Tony and the other missing children back within the next forty-eight hours.

"Here's a bag with some clothes and a wig to help you blend in, and a company card—use it. And remember, if anything happens, you transport out of there and back to headquarters."

"I will," I tell him. I take the card from him and shove it in my pocket next to my mom's coin, and I swing the backpack over one shoulder.

He pulls up another holographic image. A dense park appears on the screen along with a map beside it. "This is where you are going to transport to. It's three in the morning there, so it should be pretty deserted."

I study both pictures, trying to form the image in my mind.

"You've got your phone?" he asks.

"Yes," I say, patting my jeans.

"Good, now get going," he says, and I look at the image one more time before I close my eyes.

I make a quick stop to change, put on the ridiculous black wig, and then I'm off to Myanmar.

I LIE on the bed of my seriously nicer-than-I-expected hotel room. There isn't much going on at four in the morning, and I would stick out like a sore thumb anyways if I was walking the streets. I want to find Tony, and this kills me, but I know I've got to be smart about this. So I focus on the room instead. It's cute with the purple throw blanket at the end of the bed. And it has a stocked mini bar with snacks. I didn't realize how hungry I was until I got in here and sat down. But by far the best thing is the view; it's amazing. I've got an unobstructed view of the Shwedagon Pagoda, and even in the early morning hours, before the sun has risen, it shines.

But I've got a while before I can leave the hotel room. And thank-fully that should give me enough time that the people hanging out in the park will no longer be there. When I first transported here, I realized right away that Mr. Smith was wrong. It wasn't a deserted place; there were actually a bunch of people walking through the park.

People spotted me right away and started shouting in a language I've never heard before. Thankfully it was still dark, so I was able to run fast and use the trees as cover. When I got to the hotel, I got a lot of looks. Not many young American girls travel to Asia alone, but thankfully now that I know where my room is, I can come and go by transporting.

I close my eyes, promising myself it'll only be for a minute.

BRIGHT LIGHT SHINING through my room is what finally wakes me. Man, that temple acts like a laser beam when the sun hits it just right. I shade my eyes a bit and sit up. I look at the bedside table; it's already ten. I jump out of the bed, cursing myself for sleeping that long. The rest of the crew still won't be here for a while, but I might as well go see if I can find anything.

After a quick stop to the bathroom and an outfit change that includes my lovely wig, I'm ready to go search. I look out the window, trying to pinpoint where I can transport to, but there's too much going on. Carts, cars, animals, and people line the streets. I don't know the area and I cannot get caught. Guess I'll be walking by the front desk again.

I take the elevator down and as I walk by front desk, the woman behind it calls out what sounds like "min-ga-la-ba." I've got no clue what that means, but she's smiling, so I smile back and wave.

I step out into the mid-morning sun. The air is warm, but without humidity. It feels amazing. When I left D.C. it was freezing, so this is awesome. I walk down a busy street, heading for the Buddhist temple. The brochure at the hotel said it was only a three-minute walk. I look at my phone and study the pictures Mr. Smith sent me. I don't know if they'll help, but at least it's something.

I do my best to scan faces as I walk, but it's hard to stay focused with all the smells, sounds, and colors. This is such a colorful place; it's beautiful. I wish I was here for a different reason. Tony would probably point out everything I can't see.

And it's that thought that helps me refocus. I need Tony. I want him to show me all the things I'm missing out on. I want to hear his laugh. I want to watch his face light up. I need to make sure he's going to be okay.

People call out greetings to me as I pass, but I just keep smiling and waving. It sucks being in a place and not knowing the language. Most of these people sound generally nice, but they could be cursing me out and I'd have no clue. It'd also be nice to ask if they've seen anyone in the pictures I've got.

I turn a corner and stop in my tracks. In front of me is one of the entrances to the Shwedagon Pagoda, and it's crazy. Two white-and-gold plated dragons stand guard on either side of the gate, and these guys are like three stories tall. And it's not just a plain metal gate they're guarding. No, this is an intricate gold-and-green tiered building that comes to a fine point at the top. What's really cool is that it lines up perfectly with the temple behind it, almost like it could nestle into it.

The street leading up to the gate is full of vendors with small, umbrella-covered carts and stalls. Tons of people fill the area, walking from one stall to another, others yelling for people to come check out their wares. It's a little overwhelming, because I don't know how I'm going to spot anyone in this crowd while staying somewhat hidden. Maybe if I can get higher.

I make my way to one of the dragons guarding the gate. People yell at me as I pass, and I just keep a smile on my face. Hopefully I don't stick out like a sore thumb but just looking like a typical tourist. I finally make it to the bottom of the stairs, and they are super ornate with their carved stone railings. My head tips back so I can see the top of the dragons in front of me; if it's possible, being this close makes them even larger.

I walk up the steps, listening to people talking. I can't make it out, but it sounds like there are so many more different sounds than in the English language. I get to the top and look inside. It's not an ordinary gate, but a golden passageway with shops. The ceiling is a beautiful carved wood and the sides are lined with carved golden pillars. There's so much color in here, with the murals near the ceilings and different items people are selling. It's hard not to just stand there and gawk at everything, but maybe another time I can come back here.

I walk back outside and stand next to a tall board covered in a map. A few other people stand around it, and I turn my head and scan the busy market crowd below. This is going to take forever.

TWENTY-SIX

Three hours. I moved around that market for three hours. And I couldn't stay in one place, because if I lingered too long, people started looking at me like I was going to rob them. Last thing I need is for someone to call the police.

But I'm still here, hanging out at the market, and seriously trying to decide if I should just go back to the hotel room. It's warm and I'm hungry. I start heading away from temple, because there are a ton more touristy spots here. As I near the end of the row, a face makes me pause. I rub my eyes, because there's no way I'm seeing the man walking down the street. Henderson. I haven't seen or heard of him since he tried to kidnap me at the cabin. How did he get away from headquarters? Did the traitor release some of the people in containment? Did he not even make it to headquarters?

Should I call this in? But what if I lose him? He starts walking a little faster and that makes my decision for me; I'll call after I figure out where he's going.

I turn and walk parallel with him, but I keep stopping every now and again at a stall. There's a really good chance that I'm being super obvious.

I pick up a bracelet and the lady asks me something. "It's beautiful," I tell her, putting it back as my eyes stray to Henderson.

He turns down another street, and I start to follow after him, but pause. If I remember right, his power was the duplicate himself. What if that's a decoy? I look around quickly, searching the crowd, but I don't see anyone that resembles him.

I take off after him, trying to walk quickly but casually, and it's actually a really hard thing to do. I don't think I'll ever really make it as a spy. At least this isn't super cliché with him going down a dark alley, because I have no plans to follow him down that just so he can jump out and attack me.

He turns another corner, and thankfully there are a lot of people walking around. A bus drives by and people hang out the windows, taking photos of the temple on cell phones. A couple stands to the side of the road and points at a map.

Henderson keeps walking, like he knows exactly where to go. He's been here for a while. I follow far behind him for ten minutes before he turns again and I lose sight of him in the crowd. When I get closer to where I last saw him, I come to a complete stop.

The place he turned into has a gate barring the way, and over the top is a metal arch with the words *Emperor of India*. I stumble back a bit, my heart racing in my chest. My eyes take in the building, with the large courtyard and teal walls. This is the place my mom showed me in my dream.

I'd chalked up Brazil to my mind already knowing that was where Tiberius was and it just filtering into my dreams. But this? This actually terrifies me. Because these dreams don't feel like dreams anymore, but I don't know what they are or who's controlling them.

I look around for Henderson, but he's disappeared. I walk through the gate and into the courtyard. I have no clue what this place is. It's quiet though, completely different from the market. I head to the side of the main building, just like my mom showed me.

That secret door has got to be there; otherwise why else did she show me this place?

I walk alongside the wall and run my hand over the spot she showed me. Nothing happens, but when I move my hand a little to the left, there's a soft snick, and a door opens in the wall. My adrenaline surges, but I take a deep breath and I stick my head partially inside the open door. A stairwell descends into darkness. I take a tentative step inside, but after the first few stairs I can't see anything else. And I can't tell if the noises I'm hearing are from outside or down below. But there's a definite smell reaching my nose, and it's gross enough that I need to turn my head while I dry heave. *That. Is. Foul.* It smells like raw sewage mixed with pond water and moth balls, all to form a hot soup. My whole body cringes as I get another whiff.

I want to see if Henderson is down there, but I'm afraid I'll puke or tip them off and they'll move Tony before I can help.

I check my phone again. The rest of the team should be here in four more hours. So for now I've got to hang out until they get here. I quietly back out of there and softly close the door, sealing in the vomit-inducing stench, and leave the compound. I won't go far, and hopefully this next chunk of time will fly by.

"FINALLY," I mutter under my breath as I catch sight of Gregory, Xavier, and Raven as they round a corner.

I stand from the park bench that has been my home for the past hour. The sun set a long time ago, and I've been sitting here hiding in the dark. I could have transported back to the hotel room, but I was afraid I'd miss someone else coming or going.

Gregory reaches me first and hooks an arm around my waist. He leans down and presses a quick kiss to my cheek.

"Uhh..."

"Don't worry. With their powers, they already know," he tells me, his voice making butterflies take flight in my stomach.

"Okay, so, uh, how was the flight?" I ask, still not sure how to navigate this.

"Long," Xavier says.

Gregory hugs me closer and I feel something poking out of his side underneath his jacket. I reach my hand up, but he gently pushes my hand back down. "We're all carrying," he tells me.

Carrying? Oh. *Oh.* Good thing they flew a private plane here, because there's no way they'd get those guns through security.

"We already talked with Mr. Smith, but tell us what you found?" Gregory asks me.

"Henderson is here," I tell Gregory.

"What?" he asks, totally taken back.

"That's how I found this place; I followed him."

"How's that even possible?" he asks himself.

Xavier gives me a questioning look, and I tell him about the incident at the cabin.

As I start to fill them in on what happened after finding Henderson, Raven walks over to a nearby tree. A bird hops down and lands on her shoulder. I'll never get used to that. I turn back to the guys and tell them everything, except for the dreams.

We walk back to where I found the hidden the door. Xavier steps around me and puts his hand on the door. The three of us stand there holding our breath. I'm almost a hundred percent sure Tony is down there, but you never know.

"He's here, but the kids aren't," Xavier tells us, keeping his voice soft.

My heart picks up and I start rocking back and forth. "Well, let's go get him," I say when no one moves. "Maybe he knows where they're keeping all the kids."

He moves his hand to a different spot on the door. "There are about seven people down there, not including Tony," Xavier says.

Gregory's jaw tightens. "It's not the best odds," Gregory says, his voice sounding unsure.

"Yeah, but we all have powers," I tell them.

"And so do they, and theirs are active powers, whereas ours are more passive," Raven reminds me, putting a gentle hand on my shoulder.

"Remember Henderson can multiply himself. So we'd be dealing with eleven people instead of seven," Gregory cautions.

"Then we take him out first," I tell him, because it's the obvious first step.

"How do you expect us to find him?"

I choose to ignore that question from Gregory and turn back to Raven. Because maybe their powers don't have to be passive.

"Can you like, call a rat up here and see if it can do a little recon for us?" I ask her.

Her face looks puzzled. "I've never done that before."

"Well, no time like now to give it a try," I tell her, ushering her forward.

She opens the door and we all take a step back at the stench. I pull my shirt up to cover my nose, but it's not really helping. Raven coughs a few times and bends down and we wait. After a few minutes when nothing happens, I lean forward and place my hand on her arm. Maybe I can enhance her like Tiberius, just not so much to knock her out. She turns at the touch to her arm. "Try again," I urge her.

I focus on one rat coming and helping us. Hopefully if I think of just one, that's all that'll come. Because if a bunch start pouring out of that doorway, it's going to take everything not to run screaming.

We hear it before we see it. And as soon as it comes into view I pray there aren't any more, because this thing is larger than a Barbie doll. The rat and Raven stare at each other. Man, I hope that thing's not carrying the plague. It scurries away and Raven stands, turning to face us.

"He said there are a bunch of people down there, but he'll see if the path is clear. Luckily rats are everywhere here, so he'll probably go unnoticed," she tells us.

"Be prepared to call a horde of rats to our rescue," I tell her, and she laughs, but I'm not kidding.

The rat makes it back quickly and we follow it into the dark stairwell. The smell in here is five times worse. I'm pretty sure someone left a bunch of decomposing bodies in a barrel of piss. What is this place? Is this where the world empties their septic tanks?

We take our time slowly walking down the stairs, trying not to make any sound. Gregory takes the lead so he can read any mind that comes close enough. Raven and I take the middle, with Xavier bringing up the rear.

Gregory holds his hand up and we all stop, crouching low. He closes his eyes; I scoot forward and place my hand in his. Someday I'll have to tell him about my enhancing power, but for now I'll let him think I'm showing him support.

As he grips my hand tighter, I start to hear male voices. I look around, but it's just us. And then it registers: I can hear what he's hearing. That has *never* happened before. I drop his hand quickly like it burned me, and Raven looks at me with concern. But I just shake my head. I couldn't make out any words, but it makes my skin crawl just from the sound.

Gregory's eyes open and he motions for us to scoot closer. We all shove together into a squashed circle. "No one knows we're here. So that's a plus, but I'm not sure how we're going to get Tony out."

When the rat from earlier—I'm assuming it's the same rat—runs over to Raven, we all trade looks.

The rats.

"What if we use the rats as a distraction?" I ask.

Gregory motions for me to continue. "I know there are thousands upon thousands of rats in this city. What if Raven called as many as she could? Like sent out a distress beacon? It could give us our chance to get Tony out of here."

Raven shakes her head and goes to open her mouth, but I put a hand on her arm. "Try, please," I beg her.

"Okay," she says.

"Let's do it," Gregory says, "We're real close to them now. Raven, see if you can tell the rats to swarm whoever is standing and isn't us. Xavier, try and disarm anyone that attacks, and do your best not to use lethal force. Becca, you search for Tony."

We all nod our heads. Raven looks at the rat near her and I grab her arm, pretending I need balance. But I focus whatever enhancing ability I have and pump it into Raven, and pray it works.

The screams that start to filter up the stairs will probably haunt my dreams for years.

TWENTY-SEVEN

We walk slowly down the dark hallway and emerge upon a large open area that's erupted in pure chaos. Hundreds of rats swarm the room. They fight one another as they claw up anyone standing. Arms are flailing in the air. The screams mixed with the noise of the biting rats chill me to the bone. A body drops to the floor, and as the rats disperse, Sariah's form comes into view. Her hair is matted in blood, and her clothes look like they went through a wood chipper. Her arms are bloody and ravaged. Bile rises up the back of my throat, but it's stemmed by the sight of the rise and fall of her chest.

At the moment, we go unnoticed in the confusion. Another body drops, and as soon as it's down the rats converge on someone else. Fire emerges from around the bend at the far end of the room. Do they have a freaking flame thrower?

The rats don't run from the flames, though; they run straight into them, trying to get to whoever is behind it. "Daemon." Raven says the name on a whisper. *Who?* My head whips to her. Her eyes are filled with tears, and her hand is clenched against her chest.

The smell of burnt hair and cooked meat reaches my nose.

Gregory's voice shakes us all into action. "We've got to find Tony and get out of here. Now!"

I search the room. He's got to be here somewhere. The flames get closer, snagging my attention. They're not coming from a flame thrower; they're coming out of a pair of hands. Everything about the man attached to those hands is dark: his clothes, skin, hair—but as his eyes turn towards us, I take a breath, because they're so green they shine. He keeps the flames going, causing rats to fall charred to the floor before they even have a chance to touch him. He falters for a second when he locks gazes with Raven, allowing one of the rats to sneak in and bite his leg. He blasts it with fire, and just the rat burns; his clothes stay virtually intact.

"Becca! Find Tony!" Gregory yells again, and I run to the other side of the room.

I finally spot him, a lump in the corner with what smells like raw sewage. I drop to my knees next to his broken body. Behind me, I hear the pounding of human flesh and grunts of pain. I quickly look over my shoulder. Most of the rats have been cooked. We don't have much time.

I push the overgrown, greasy hair out of Tony's face. His nose is swollen and terribly crooked, blood still slowly trickling out of it. They must have broken it recently. The rest of his face is layered in both fresh and old bruises. I pick up his hand they took the finger from. The area is an angry red and oozing puss. What else did they do to him? His chest rises and falls in shallow breaths. His forehead is covered in sweat, but he doesn't even twitch as I drag him into my lap.

My head jerks to the left at the sound of a gunshot. More people are flooding into the room to join the fight. I need to get Tony out of here.

I scan the room, looking for help. I can't carry him myself. I find Gregory fighting off two guys. Raven's called more rats into the battle.

Xavier starts running across the room towards me, but he's tackled to the ground. No one can help me. I look back down at what's left of Tony. If we don't leave, he's going to die. I won't lose him like Ania.

A crazy plan spreads rapidly through my mind. I can transport him. I know it almost killed him the last time I did it, but I can't leave him here. But where am I going to take him? I can't bring him back to headquarters. What if the traitor finds him?

Tiberius. He'll be able to help. I quickly take out one of my earrings out and lock my eyes and mind onto Gregory. *Gregory, I'm going to transport Tony out of here. He's going to die if we stay.*

"Becca!" Gregory screams my name as he punches a man in the face.

Get everyone out of here!

"Raven, more rats!" I scream at her. She doesn't look my way, just floods the area with more creatures, creating another wave of chaos.

"The stairs!" Gregory yells, causing Xavier and Raven to make a break for it.

"What about Becca?!" Xavier makes to run for me, but Gregory grabs him by the arm.

"She's leaving too," Gregory screams over the noise, and pulls him to the stairs.

I put my earrings back in, and then look back at Tony's face and wrap my arms tight around him. Maybe if I block out everything and focus on enhancing the transport, the two of us can arrive whole at Tiberius's house. It could work. I close my arms tighter around him and picture Tony's smiling face looking back at me on the roof of the cabin. I see him in my arms now and I focus on the feel under my fingertips. The breath of his shoulders, the feel of his torn shirt.

I start rocking us, feeling the weight of him on me. I picture Tiberius's home, the couch in his living room. In my mind I'm sitting on that couch, with Tony still in my arms, feeling his body against mine. I keep rocking us and projecting those images over and over in my mind, squeezing my eyes shut as I feel the pull of the transport.

A child's scream blasts my eardrums. I open my eyes to see Bronia staring at me from across the couch. What is she doing here? I look around to make sure I transported to the right house. This is Tiberius's living room.

She leans closer to me. "Becca?" she asks in a scared voice.

I nod my head and it sends her running from the room. "JaJa, come quick, it's Becca and a man!"

Man? Tony! I look down at his face. He's too still. I check his pulse at his neck—

nothing. I climb out from underneath him, my knees hitting the hard floor. I lean over him and place my ear to his chest. I can't hear anything. "Come on, Tony!" I yell, pushing on his chest.

"Out of the way, Becca," Walter says as he shoves me back.

He takes a stethoscope out of a bag, throws it on, and places it against Tony's chest. Complete silence engulfs the room.

He slumps a little bit. "There's a pulse, it's faint. But by the look of him he's got a lot going wrong. He needs fluids right away. And I need blankets to get him warm," Walter says, but it takes me a second to realize he's not talking to me.

I look over my shoulder. Tiberius is right behind me and Lucy is farther back, with Bronia in her arms. But at Walter's words, Tiberius takes off from the room, hopefully following Walter's orders.

"Where did you find this *chłopiec*?" he asks, slipping into Polish as he lifts up Tony's eyelids, searching for something that only people in the medical field seem to know about.

"In raw sewage, underneath a building in Myanmar," I tell him in a hollow voice.

A soft gasp comes from behind me. "Let's go make some broth for him when he wakes up," I hear Lucy hastily tell Bronia.

As soon as they leave, I lay a hand on Walter's arm. He stops his examination and looks at me. "He was tortured. I don't know how much, but they sent us a finger in the mail the other day. I shouldn't have transported him. He could still die because of me, but I couldn't leave him there." My voice breaks on the last couple of words.

He reaches a hand out and cups my cheek. "You did well. Ania would be proud," he says, and a sob rips out of me. He wraps one arm around me while he keeps his hand on Tony's wrist. "Let it out," he tells me, sounding like my own grandpa.

And I do. I sob into his shoulder. My body starts to shake as it comes down off the adrenaline I was functioning on. "Breathe," he tells me. I take in shuddering breaths.

The room's silence is broken when Tiberius comes rushing back in, his arms full of stuff. I wipe my face off on my sleeve.

"Let's get him on the table," Walter says, motioning towards the dining room table. We all grab a part of him and bring him over, gently setting him down.

I scoot out of the way so Tiberius and Walter can start working on Tony. Tiberius covers him with blankets while Walter starts putting in an IV. I'm amazed at how quick and efficient they are, but it's probably not the first time either has had to deal with this.

Walter lifts up Tony's hand that's missing part of a finger. It's gruesome; there's no other way to describe it. And from the looks of the jagged skin, it wasn't a clean cut. "The antibiotics in the IV should clear this up, but I need to clean it out," Walter tells us.

"At least he's still unconscious," I say, watching his still form.

"But he might not stay that way when I start," Walter cautions me. He turns to look at Tiberius. "You'll need to be ready to hold him down. I'm going to go get a few other things. I'll be right back."

He leaves the room and Tiberius turns to me. "Does anyone know you're here?" he asks.

"No. I couldn't bring him to headquarters. What if they got to him there? Here was the safest place." I run my hands over my thighs, and stop when I feel the outline of my phone. I look up at Tiberius, fear seizing me.

"My cell," I rasp the words out, bringing the phone out my pocket, dropping it like it burned me.

"It's okay. Lucy has the whole place wired to scramble cell signals. And as long as you transported directly here, you'll be fine," he tells me, and his assurance lightens me, but only a little. I put the phone back in my pocket.

"You can't go back. It's getting to dangerous," he says, his voice gentle.

"I can't just disappear," I tell him. "We didn't find the kids. And what would happen to my grandparents if I left? They need me. They're probably waiting for me right now." Not to mention Gregory, but I can't tell Tiberius about him.

"Tony's in no condition to leave, and probably won't be for weeks. What do you think will happen when you go back without him?" His words are soft, like he's trying not to rile me.

"I haven't thought that far ahead yet. I just couldn't leave him there." I have no clue what to do. But staying isn't an option. "I can't transport him again; he won't survive that," I tell him.

Our conversation stops when Walter comes back in carrying a large black bag. He drops it next to Tony. "Get ready to hold him by the shoulders," he tells Tiberius as he takes bandages, a scalpel, and tweezers out of his bag.

"I didn't know you were a doctor," I say, watching him riffle through his bag.

"I'm not,"—I suck in a breath—"at least not in America. I was one in Poland, though." I let the breath out slowly.

I scoot around the table so I'm closer to Tony's good hand and out of the way. Walter pulls on rubber gloves and gently takes Tony's injured hand. He moves it around. "I'm going to need to cut the skin to drain the infection and then flush it out," he tells us.

Tiberius gently puts pressure on Tony's shoulder. I grab his good hand and watch Walter pull out his tools. "I wish I could numb him, but I just don't have that on me," he tells us like he's apologizing.

Walter takes his scalpel and makes a small cut on what's left of Tony's finger. Tony flinches and Tiberius pushes down more on his shoulders.

"Shh. You're okay, I'm here with you," I say into his ear. I doubt he can actually hear anything I say, but *I* need him to know that.

Walter takes a syringe out and removes the needle. He fills it up and starts cleaning out the wound. The smell alone makes me want to gag, but I hold back. Walter takes tweezers and that's when I turn my head and focus on Tony's face. I can't watch anymore. I hold his hand and stroke his temple. I hope this gives him some comfort.

He starts to moan.

"Keep talking to him," Walter tells me.

So I do. I tell him about Raven and her Snow White-like talent. I tell him about the creepy school I had to transport to. I tell him about how I want to sit on a roof again with him and look at astronauts picking their noses. The last one gets a chuckle out of Tiberius. But the one thing I keep saying to him over and over again is how much I need to see his smile and hear his voice.

"All done," Walter says. I look over and Walter's removing his gloves. "Hopefully with the antibiotics and the wound cleaned, we won't have to worry about the infection spreading."

I place Tony's hand by his side and step back from the table. "I can't stay," I tell them. "I'll just tell Mr. Smith he's somewhere safe."

"That won't work and you know it." Tiberius's words are trying to urge me to see reason, and stay.

"What about my grandparents?" I ask.

"They can come here," Tiberius says without missing a beat.

I can't imagine my grandmother here. And I don't know what it would take to convince them to leave their home and everything they know. I rub both hands over my face. Walter steps forward and puts a hand on my shoulder. "Go back to your team in Myanmar. Tell them you brought him to me; they don't need to know where. Gregory knows I was a doctor in Poland. It'll take time to get to my home to check if I'm there. Go to your grandparents and see if they'll leave. You can't stay at Project Lightning, Becca. You aren't safe there anymore."

"I'm not worried about that. They can't hold me anywhere. But what about the kids? This is the closest we've come to finding them. I won't lose this chance. They can't transport to safety like I can."

Tiberius steps closer to us. "We'll find them. And we won't stop until we do." His words are a vow, and I trust him on that. But I feel like we're running on borrowed time. We need to find these kids, and soon.

"I need to help them figure out who's behind all of this and make sure my grandparents are protected. But I'll be back," I tell them.

TWENTY-EIGHT

I transport into my hotel room, and before I even open my eyes I'm being picked up clear off my feet. "Are you all right? Where the hell did you go?" Gregory's voice is harsh, but I still throw my arms around him, glad he made it out safely.

I look over his shoulder. Xavier and Raven both sit on the bed looking exhausted, but Raven seems worse. She has a haunted look in her eyes, but before I can ask her if she's okay, Gregory takes my attention. "Where's Tony?" he asks as he steps back and looks at my face.

"With Walter," I tell him, and he nods his head.

"Walter?" Xavier asks, his eyebrows pulling together.

"Ania's dad. He's a doctor," Gregory tells them without looking away from me.

"Did you call Mr. Smith?" I ask, my nerves ratcheting high.

"No, I wanted to wait and see where you went, but I was about to because you weren't answering your phone," he says, searching my face.

"I'm sorry," I tell him, doing my best not to avert my eyes.

His face pulls into a pinched expression and I know he's frustrated because he can't hear my thoughts. He stares at me for a moment longer and then pulls out his phone. He presses the speaker and puts it down on the bed.

"Report," Mr. Smith says in lieu of a greeting.

Gregory recounts what we found underneath the building in Myanmar, but he fails to mention the rats or the guy with flames. "Henderson is here," Gregory tells him.

"What?" Mr. Smith barks out.

"Someone must have snuck him out," Gregory says.

Mr. Smith lets out a long, frustrated sigh. "I'll have to look into it. But what about the children?"

Everyone seems to slump more with that question. "There was no sign of them," Gregory says.

"Tony?" Mr. Smith asks, his voice rising, anxiety starting to bleed through.

Everyone looks at me. "I transported him—"

"You did what?!" Mr. Smith shouts into the phone, making me want to take a step back even though he isn't here.

"I brought him to Walter," I tell him.

"What were you thinking?" He roars out the question, and it causes my whole body to tense. I don't care that I made a risky decision; it was the right one. And his tone is seriously pissing me off, because he wasn't there. He didn't see the shape Tony was in—still is in.

"I didn't want to leave him there to die in filth!"

Gregory grabs me back into his chest. My breathing is coming fast and my body feels like a live wire. He tries to whisper calming words into my ear, but I can't hear him over the hammering of my heart.

"And why didn't you bring him back here?" he asks the question like I'm stupid, but I've got no problem firing back on this one.

"Last time I checked, we haven't found the traitor yet. I wasn't about to put him right back in harm's way. Sariah's already played all

THE BLESSED MANY   195

of us for a fool; I'm not letting anything else happen to him." I know I'm being insubordinate, but I just don't care anymore.

"Did he tell you anything?" he asks, sounding completely exasperated with me.

"No. He didn't even wake up when Walter had to cut into his infected finger to flush the wound."

Raven turns a little green at my comments. That turns her stomach, but hundreds of rats chewing on people doesn't?

"We need to interview him right away. Gregory, I need you heading towards him," Mr. Smith orders.

Gregory looks at me like he just realized that I didn't actually tell him where Tony is. He hesitates answering.

"Gregory?" Mr. Smith asks.

"I...uh..." He looks at me, his hands raised, but I keep my mouth shut.

"Do you have a problem talking with him?" Mr. Smith asks.

He releases a heavy sigh when I still won't give up any information. "I don't know where he is, sir," Gregory finally tells him.

"Isn't he with Walter?" Mr. Smith asks, sounding confused.

"He is," I say, but I can't look at anyone in the room, because I know what question is coming next.

"Where are they?" he asks.

I look down at the floor. "I can't tell you," I say, and the whole room freezes. Mr. Smith doesn't say anything. I don't even think I hear him breathe. I look up and see Raven's eyes widen.

"Why?" It's one word, but even though he's halfway across the world and on the phone, he says that word with such rage.

I swallow down my nerves before I piss him off even more. "Walter took Bronia into hiding." Gregory hangs his head and Xavier lets out a low whistle. "He asked to stay that way. I won't betray his trust, and you shouldn't either. I can transport back there any time and talk to Tony. Let him stay somewhere safe, at least until you find the traitor and he heals," I basically beg him.

I keep looking at the phone, thinking he hung up, because the length of silence on his end is freaking me out. I don't know how Mr. Smith is going to react. I finally scan the room, and three sets of wide eyes watch me.

"I agree." We all release a simultaneous breath. "He'll be safe with Walter. Gregory, take me off speaker."

Gregory picks up the phone and walks to a corner of the room. "That felt too easy, right?" I ask Raven and Xavier.

"I don't know," Xavier tells me, his voice low. "You realize, though that the next time you see Mr. Smith, he'll ask you these questions in person?"

"I know," I tell him. I'll just have to figure out a way around that.

Gregory walks back over to us, looking extremely tired. "He wants us to stay here. See if we can go back and check the area for clues as to where the kids are."

"Won't they be waiting for us? They saw all of us," I say.

"I doubt they saw us with all the chaos around the rats and fire," Gregory tells me.

Well, there's one person that knows Raven was there. But no one is talking about the guy with the fire, so I guess I shouldn't mention her calling Daemon's name.

"I can transport to the stairwell real quick and tell you if anyone's there," I offer.

Gregory hesitates and nods his head reluctantly. In the blink of an eye I'm gone.

The stench is like a close-fisted punch to the face. Charred meat, burnt hair, and sewage assault my poor sinuses. Bile pools in my mouth, but I fight through the nausea. I bring my shirt up to cover my mouth and nose. It doesn't do much, but it's a little bit better, and I'll take that.

I crouch on the stairs and listen. Silence greets me. There isn't even the sound of rats nearby. But I wait for a bit longer, frozen on the step. After a few minutes of nothing, I slowly creep the rest of the way down.

It's a burned shell. All that's left is ash. Blood stains some of the walls. This place looks like the set of a horror movie. But thankfully, no one is here.

I transport back to the hotel room.

"No one there's. And not much is left of the place either," I tell them.

"Let's go see what we can find," Gregory says.

We head back over and instead of slowly descending the stairs, we take them two at time. "Raven, talk with the rats. Xavier, see what you can find out," Gregory orders.

Gregory and I stand off to the side while the other two get to work. "Are you going to tell me where they are?" Gregory asks, turning into me.

"I can't." It pains me to say that to him, but if he wants me to trust him, he's got to trust me on this.

He makes a noise of frustration, mixed with understanding. He plants his hands on his hips and looks to the floor as he takes deep breaths. "How was he?" he asks me.

"In really rough shape." The image of Tony's lifeless body plays on repeat in my mind. "I'll go check on him soon and see if he's conscious."

"Got them," Xavier calls out. We rush over to where he's kneeling on the ground. "There's a warehouse three miles from here. They're holding the kids there and—" He makes a pained noise and looks up at us.

"What is it?" I ask.

"From what they're saying—they keep calling the warehouse 'the laboratory.' I think they're doing testing on the kids." His voice shakes on the last word, and it worries me. Because with all that Xavier has gone through, this is the first time I've seen him show fear.

"Now's the perfect time to go there," Gregory says. "They're all injured. We don't have time to waste. We need to move on this now."

"Do we need to call Mr. Smith?" Raven asks.

"We'll brief him after everyone's safe," Gregory says, and I grab him by the arm.

"We're getting those kids out," I say. "And afterward...we're burning that place to the ground."

I may be talking to Gregory, but everyone nods their heads in agreement. It could have been one of us tortured or experimented on. It could have been Bronia or Poppy. We can't let what happened to Lucy happen to them.

TWENTY-NINE

We move fast through the streets of Yangon. Some stop to watch us rush past, but most are too busy with their own lives. It takes us no time to reach the outskirts of the city, where the building is located. It looks like any other warehouse: metal siding, rust at the bottom with weeds desperately trying to find every crack to spring through, and trash strewn about.

"How many inside?" Xavier asks, his focus on Gregory.

Gregory closes his eyes. "Three kids, everyone from earlier, and another man." His face pales. "Those kids are in pain."

"Let's go get them," I say, starting to move, but Gregory grabs my arm.

"We need a plan," he says.

"Most of them are injured. If we wait too long they'll have more backup," I say, motioning to the watch on his wrist.

"Daemon wasn't injured," Raven says in a small voice.

"Daemon?" I ask, and I know who she's talking about, but I want her to tell us.

"Guy with the fire," Xavier says, bailing her out. "I agree with

Gregory: we need a plan. Can you tell by their thoughts where the kids are located in the building?"

"I'm not sure—" Gregory starts to say, but I butt right in. "Try," I tell him and grab his hand.

He closes his eyes and his mouth purses. "It looks like the kids are to the left, and the others are towards the front at the right."

We make our way slowly around the building and stop when Gregory does. There aren't any doors, but above us is a window that none of us are going to fit through. "Are you sure it's just the kids back here?" I ask, eyeing the window.

He nods.

"What if I transport in and get the kids through the window for you to catch below?" I ask.

Gregory looks at the window and back at me. He bites his lip and starts shaking his head. But I've got to do this, and I'll do it with or without him. "I'll be quick," I promise.

He squeezes my hand. "Be careful and be quiet," he tells me.

I have no clue what's on the other side of this metal wall, but I'm hoping that if I'm just transporting a few feet it won't make a difference. I close my eyes and picture myself ten feet in front of me.

I open my eyes and reach out to snatch the IV pole I transported into. My fingers wrap around the cold metal right before it hits the ground. I slowly stand it back up and take a calming breath. That would have been awful.

I turn to the room and three pair of wide eyes watch me. I put my finger to my lips. I inspect the room for the closest door. Thank goodness it's shut. I turn back and survey the room. Two young boys and a girl are each strapped down to a bed, their little bodies covered in small hospital gowns. Their eyes track me, but none of them make a sound or move. And it all just makes my heart ache.

I walk over to the closest little boy. He's maybe five, with dark brown hair and large brown eyes. He's got IVs poking out of each arm. I bend close to his ear. "My name is Becca, and I'm going to get you out of here." I stand and gaze back at him, but he doesn't say anything, just stares. "Blink twice if you can hear me."

His eyes slowly close two times. Are they paralyzed? I shake my head. It doesn't matter, because I can feel a clock ticking down and I need to move.

I walk over to the other two and tell them the same thing. Both look at me with hope shining through. The little girl's green eyes start to well with tears. "I've got to take the needles out. Okay?" I ask her, and she blinks twice.

I grab a tissue nearby to hide what I'm about to do. My stomach knots as I slowly remove the tape from her arm. She doesn't even twitch, but her eyes close. I slide out the first needle, praying that she's not feeling pain from it. As soon as it's out I hold the tissue over her arm to stop the bleeding. All right, I did it. Only have to do it five more times.

I quickly move around the room, pulling out all the IVs while listening for anyone coming. So far so good.

I walk back to the first little boy. "Blink once for no, two for yes. Can you move at all?" I ask.

He blinks once.

I look up at the window above; I need to feed them through that. I search the room and in the corner a chair rests against the wall. I pick it up and rush it under the window. I climb it slowly and reach for the latch. As I push it open, it creaks and I freeze. They have to have heard that. I stand frozen on the chair, waiting for the door to open, but nothing happens. I open it as far as it'll go.

I get back down and look at the little boy. "I'm going to pick you up, okay?"

He blinks twice.

I lift him in my arms and he seems way too light. We scramble onto the chair and I boost him higher up in my arms. I angle his bare little feet out and slowly lower him down. Xavier and Gregory wait below and they grab onto his legs. As his face comes close to mine, I watch tears slide down his cheeks. The guys grab him from below and pass him off to Raven. She cradles him to her chest.

The next boy goes much the same, but as I'm picking up the little girl, I hear footsteps approaching. Her eyes widen and I move faster up onto the chair and swing her legs out the window. The guys are grabbing her from below when I hear the footsteps stop next to the door and a muffled exchange. I hang my head out the window. "Hurry out of here, someone's coming. I'll meet you back at the hotel," I tell him.

Gregory pauses with the little girl in his arms, but I wave him off.

I turn around and scan the room. I'm not leaving until I do some damage. In the far corner is a chemistry set-up just like Dex is using at headquarters. I rush over to it and spot a Bunsen burner sitting among a microscope, glass jars, and other things. I light the burner and hurry over to the closest bed and grab the sheet.

The knob on the door starts to turn and I place a corner of the sheet under the flame. It quickly ignites and I rush over the other beds, catching the sheets on fire as well.

"Do you smell that?" a man's deep voice asks.

I'm out of time, but I throw the burning sheet on the floor next to computer. I grab whatever I can find and start throwing it onto the fast-catching flames. The room is quickly filling with smoke and flames. I pull my shirt over my nose.

"Hey!" I hear someone scream at me from far behind, but I smash whatever else I can find. I've got to destroy this place. I reach the back wall and what I see makes my soul splinter. Embryos in test tubes. What have they done?

With hacking coughs, I grab an IV pole next to me and swing it with all my might at the glass.

"No!" a man screams, closer now. Gun shots echo nearby. But they're all too late, and glass shatters, spilling liquid and other things onto the floor at my feet. A sob rips out of my throat at the loss of life I just allowed to happen. But I couldn't let them keep doing these experiments.

A hand grabs my shoulder, but I kick out, pushing them back, and I transport out of there.

I COLLAPSE onto my knees on the floor of my hotel room. I go to take a deep breath but immediately break into a coughing fit. My body shakes with each cough, and I'm sure the tears streaming down my face are leaving tracks in the soot.

The coughing finally subsides, but I stay kneeling on the floor. What were they doing to those kids? And how can these kids go on after what happened to them? And those tanks with the embryos... how can anyone be okay with any of this? Does Sariah know that she's helping people experiment on kids? Does she know that they are trying to play God in order to experiment on babies? So many questions. I just don't get any of this. The idea of them doing those things is making me physically sick.

The door to the room bursts open and in walk the rest of them, each carrying a child. I scramble from my spot on the floor and hold the door for them. "How did you get up here without anyone seeing you?" I ask.

"Back door," Gregory says as he tenderly lays the little girl on the bed. Her eyes are wide open, but they still aren't moving their bodies. "We disabled the cameras earlier, and I couldn't hear anyone's thoughts as we made our way to the room."

Raven and Xavier gently lay the two boys down. We all step back, our stares bouncing between the kids and each other. "What now?" I ask, my voice hushed because it seems right to talk that way.

"I need to call Mr. Smith and arrange for these guys to get back to their parents," Gregory says. He looks at the kids and then faces me. "What did you see in there?" he asks, his voice lowered.

Raven and Xavier exchange a confused glance, probably wondering why he doesn't just pick it from my mind. I open my mouth to tell him the horrible things I saw, but I can't get anything out. I reach up and slowly take out my earrings, setting them down on the desk beside me. I close my eyes and let the images of everything I saw and did flood my mind. Every detail, even the smallest thing, crosses before my mind's eye.

I don't realize I'm crying until I feel Gregory's warm hand on my face, wiping away the tears staining my cheeks. "I'm sorry," he says, and I think he can feel the anguish ripping through me for what I saw and did, because I see it in him.

"They need to be stopped," I tell him. I know that's not the only place they're doing experiments. I can feel that we've only seen the tip of the iceberg.

I turn around, shielding myself as I hear Gregory softly relay to the others what happened. I slip my earrings back in and do my best to re-center myself.

"I won't let them keep going this," Xavier says, his words causing me to turn. His face is set in a hard line, and he may be across the room, but I can feel his intensity like he's right next to me. We hold each other's eyes, and I know that he would have done the exact same thing I did.

Gregory's phone ringing slices through the tension in the room. I turn away from Xavier and my eyes land on the little boy I first saw when I transported into the warehouse. I squat down beside him. "Are you cold?" I ask, and he blinks once.

"We're going to get you home soon. You're safe," I say. He blinks twice. I look at the two lying next to him, their eyes tracking me. "I'll do everything I can to make sure this doesn't happen again." I try to force as much conviction into my voice as I can. They all blink twice, and it's a balm to my heart.

"We've got backup coming," Gregory says, and I turn at his words. "They're going to help us get to the plane and escort us back to headquarters. Mr. Smith wants you to transport back."

"After I see you guys to the plane," I tell him. He nods, knowing better than to argue with me.

An hour passes and the kids have been able to twitch their fingers and toes. I don't know what kind of paralytic they gave them, but it's strong.

There's a knock at the door and Gregory walks over to the door. He pauses for a moment. "This is our backup," he tells us as he answers the door.

Four men dressed in black, their faces covered with masks, enter the room. "Not suspicious at all, huh?" I ask, letting the sarcasm flow freely.

"We don't have time for chit chat; let's go," the one in front says. Something about his voice sounds familiar, but Gregory doesn't seem alarmed, so I chalk it up to nerves.

The men in black go to pick up the kids, but Xavier steps in their way. "We'll carry them." His voice is low and lethal. The man in front raises both arms up in the air and walks backwards.

I pick up the little boy with the dark hair and eyes. His fingers twitch against my arms. "Let's get you home, bud," I whisper into his ear.

We file out of the room with Gregory in the lead, listening for anyone close by. Luckily, it's a quick trip to the back alley, where a large black suburban waits for us. We load into the car, each with a child in our laps. I hope this little guy knows he's really going home.

We bump down the road and I hold him close to me. His eyes seem lighter, if that's possible, like he's excited. We travel for only ten minutes before we turn onto a dirt road that leads to an airport hangar. A lone plane sits outside, the door open with steps pulled up to it. "We're going to have you exit one at a time," one of the men tells us.

The men in black get out and pull rifles from under their seats. They move away from the car and guard both doors. Raven exits first, with Xavier getting out close behind her. Murmured words pass between Xavier and one of the armed men, but I can't hear anything except that it's terse.

Gregory leans over and lifts the boy off my lap. His lips quickly brush mine. "I'll see you soon. Be safe. I love you," he tells me, but he doesn't give me a chance to answer him back, because he's already out the door.

I exit the car and walk behind them to the plane, taking out my earrings as I try to keep up with him. My eyes scan the area, hoping they'll get in the air before anything else can happen. Raven's already walking up the stairs with Xavier right on her heels.

Gregory reaches the bottom of the stairs. "I'll see you soon," I tell him. *I love you.* He faces me fully, and his smile is blinding.

He quickly disappears into the plane, and the four men in black walk by me, heading for the stairs.

"See you later, Becca," the one who talked to me earlier says, and man, his voice is so familiar. I wish I could rip off that mask. I nod my head at him, not sure if he's still even looking at me.

They quickly board the plane, the doors closing soon after, and I walk backwards as they pull the stairs away.

THIRTY

I step back into the hangar, watching the plane taxi down the runway. My phone buzzes in my pocket with an incoming text. I pull it out, staring at the text notification. A blocked number?

You burned what was mine to the ground. It only seemed right to return the favor

What? I grip my hair at the top of my head. There's no way they could know it was me, right? Even if they did, what of mine could they have burned to the ground? I don't have any—

And then it clicks.

I transport straight into an inferno. Flames lick up the walls of my grandparent's kitchen.

"Grandpa!" I scream out his name, but I don't hear anything over the roar of the flames.

I rush through the kitchen and into the living room, searching the floors for any sign of them. But the only thing I see is my childhood home being devoured by fire. Sirens blare in the distance, but they'll be too late; there's no saving this.

"Grandma!" Why aren't they answering?

Sweat pours off me as I race through the rest of the downstairs, flames lapping at me, heat searing me. The thick black smoke clogs the air, making my throat feel like it's closing in on itself, and my eyes sting from its assault. I run up the stairs, my knuckles white as I grip the railing. "Where are you guys!?"

I burst into their room, letting the door slam into the wall. I wipe at the tears streaming down my face, trying to see better. I scan the room, but nothing is jumping out at me except for the firestorm creeping in.

I see them, lying eerily still in their bed. Time slows as I approach Grandpa's side. A chill runs up my back as I take him in. His neck is sitting at an odd angle, and dried blood marks his nose and mouth. I reach out my hand, wanting to touch him, wanting to wake him...but I can't, and I snatch my hand back to my chest. His unseeing eyes stare back at me, and I'm struck with this gut-wrenching pain. I caused this. I caused their deaths.

The firefighters' sirens blare through the windows. "I'm sorry," I tell him, my voice hoarse. I can't bring myself to look at Grandma; just the outline of her body in my peripheral makes my stomach heave. She knew nothing of this world, and yet she's paying the price for just being my grandmother.

Flames crackle as they surround us, slithering closer to the bed, destroying everything they touch. I reach for his hand, and it's still warm. My soul cracks in two. "I love you," I tell him, the agony making it impossible to say it any louder than a whisper.

I kiss my fingers and blow a kiss across him to Grandma. I can't look; I don't want to know what they've done to her.

It takes the last bit of strength I have to step back from his side. A crash echoes from downstairs, and shouting follows. They can't find me here. I reach out and grab the picture of the three of us off his nightstand and bring it to my chest, hugging it tightly.

"I love you both so much." I push the words out and transport from the room.

———

THE TREES around the side of the house shield me as I watch the firefighters try to rescue the charred remains. I don't know how long I've stood here, but enough time has passed that all my skin feels tight and the burns feel angry. They should just let it burn. There's nothing there to save anymore. Their voices drift towards me. Words keep getting tossed around: *arson, accident, murder, devastating.*

My phone buzzes again in my pocket, but I don't want to look. I can't. I want to ignore it, like the burns I can feel on my legs and arms.

It keeps buzzing. And every time I hear the sound, my fists and eyes get tighter and tighter.

After what feels like the millionth time, I can't take it anymore. I pull it out and look down at the illuminated screen. Gregory sent me a text? Shouldn't he still be in the air? Did something happen to one of the kids? I quickly open it.

You shouldn't touch what's mine

No. This can't be happening. I stagger back into a tree, the bark biting into my wounds, but I feel nothing.

I'm not done with you yet

Why do they have his phone? Who has it? Where is he?

The traitor. They got to Gregory. My legs feel like they want to give out. But another text pops up.

This is what happens when you involve yourself in things you shouldn't

The last text has two pictures. Gregory kneeling on a tile floor, blood dripping from his mouth, and his plaid shirt is torn. My heart pounds as I move my eyes from his face to a man standing behind him, holding a gun to Gregory's head. A sour taste fills my mouth.

They wouldn't hurt him. He's too valuable. Right? Isn't that what Mr. Smith said? They didn't kill Tony because of his power. Gregory is the most valuable of all of us.

My hand shakes as I try and scroll to pull up the last text, the next picture.

The phone falls to concrete below, the screen shattering on impact and turning black. But it doesn't matter, because after today,

I'll not only be haunted by the images of my grandparents; I'll have to see the picture of Gregory's lifeless body sprawled on the floor.

No.

There's no way.

A scream claws its way up my throat and blazes out of my mouth. The distant sound of people yelling briefly hits my ears, but it fades in and out as my body starts to shake, and I start to flicker. My mind begins to detach, and I welcome it.

My body goes on autopilot, like it knows there's only one place left for me to go. I close my eyes, and when I open them I'm standing in front of Tiberius's door. I stumble into it and almost instantly the door opens.

I don't know what he sees when he looks at me. I know my clothes are burned, that I reek of smoke, and that my face is covered in ash and soot. But maybe it's my eyes that cause him to take a step back. They must reflect what I feel on the inside: dead.

"What—" Tiberius starts to say, but I cut him off.

"They're all dead. I had nowhere else to go." My voice is flat, completely devoid of any emotion.

He immediately changes his facial expression. "You always have a home here," he tells me.

His words don't register. *Home* is gone. But he needs to know my plan before I can't talk anymore...

"I want to help you find more people. I want to stop whoever is taking these kids. I need to make sure no one else suffers because of what we are," I tell him, and while my words ring with conviction, all I feel is numb. I don't want to feel, because if I do, I won't be able to stop.

People start coming out of their homes, and I don't know if it's because I appeared out of thin air. Lucy walks up behind Tiberius, placing her hand on his shoulder. His eyes scan the street, looking at everyone that's staring at me. He focuses back on me.

"Have I told you what we call ourselves here?" His voice is loud and causes people to start walking towards his house.

I shake my head no, because honestly, I don't care.

More people join, welcoming looks gracing their faces.

Tiberius holds his hand out, pointing around us. "There are over seventy-five of us here with powers. Let me be the first to welcome you to being one the Blessed Many."

I turn and look at the faces surrounding us. They smile at me, hope bright in their eyes, and it makes my heart squeeze, but I squash it and let the numbness flood me. I'll help find more of them. I'll do what Grandpa would want me to do. I won't stop. We *will* become a force to reckoned with, because this Blessed Many now has me, and I'll be damned if I let another person die.

EPILOGUE

It's a river this time. The land around us is beautiful, with its lush green grasses and abundance of wildflowers. I hate it.

I don't want to be here. I don't want these dreams anymore. Where was her warning about the fire? The last images of Grandpa and Grandma come to the forefront of my mind, and my whole body buckles. And Gregory—why couldn't she give me a chance to save him, to save them all?

"Becca?" The sound of her voice is poison in my ears.

"I don't want you to visit me in my dreams anymore," I tell her, hatred dripping from every word.

I see her in my periphery, walking closer to me. "Please. You need to—"

"No!" Lightning explodes across the sky as I whip around to face her. "I'm done with this! Done with you!"

She latches on to my arm, her nails piercing my skin. "Listen! Nothing is as it seems. Look closer. You've been deceived."

The End of Book 2

ACKNOWLEDGMENTS

I may be the only one touching the computer keys, but there are so many people behind the scenes that I need to thank.

First and foremost, I'd like to thank my husband Nick, for loving me, supporting me, dealing my stress, and keeping the kids away as I tried to finish this. You're my cheerleader and I love you for it.

Next, to my children: Mena, Xander, and Robbie. I do this all for me and you. I hope you see me reaching for my dreams and hitting my goals. Always know that you can as well, the sky's the limit babies. I love you.

Emily, Sara, Tara, Camille Cheryl, Dena, and many others; thank you for your help, your words, your encouragement, and sharing the writing journey with me.

Kathy, thank you for proofreading for me, and answering my million questions. I will always beta read for you.

To the wonderful writers of ANWA. This group holds a wealth of wisdom, and I get to take part of it. I love my Red Mountain chapter.

To my editor Jana Miller. You helped me beyond measure with this book, even with the rats. Bet you can't wait for the next one, huh?

My amazing cover designer, Molly Phipps, with We Got You Covered Book Design. You created a beautiful cover yet again, and I can't wait to see what comes next.

I'd also like to thank some musicians that helped me find the right words: Billie Eilish, NF, Dashboard Confessional, The Lumineers, The Strumbellas, and many more. The music you create has greatly inspired my writing. Without your talent, I don't think I could fully realize mine.

To my parents. You raised one seriously independent daughter. And I doubt I would have taken this on if you hadn't. You filled our home with books and learning. Mom, thanks for being to read whatever I write and to give me an honest opinion. Oh and mom, I know you're just as excited for this book as I am.

Finally, to the readers. Thank you for taking on me and reading my second book.

If you liked this book, please consider leaving a review. Thanks!

ABOUT THE AUTHOR

Pam Eaton lives in the deserts of Arizona, but she'll always consider herself a New Englander at heart. She graduated from Arizona State University with degrees involving education and history. While she loves history, it'll always take a backseat to the fictional world she stumbled into as a young girl.

She lives with her husband, three kids, and two crazy but lovable labs. It's a chaotic life, but she wouldn't have it any other way. Especially since they let her read an insane amount of books, and watch way too many Food Network shows.

You can find out more at Pam's website
www.pameaton.com
Or email her peaton.ya@gmail.com

facebook.com/authorpameaton

instagram.com/author_pam_eaton

ALSO BY PAM EATON

The Extraordinary Series

An Extraordinary Few

The Blessed Many

An Army of One

Made in the USA
Middletown, DE
10 January 2021

31235625R00126